BORDERLINE

Borderline
by MARIE-SISSI LABRÈCHE

Translation from the French
by MELISSA BULL

ANVIL PRESS • VANCOUVER

Copyright © 2000 by Marie-Sissi Labrèche
Translation copyright © 2020 by Melissa Bull

Originally published in French under the same title by Les Éditions du Boréal 2000.

All rights reserved. No part of this book may be reproduced by any means without
the prior written permission of the publisher, with the exception of brief passages
in reviews. Any request for photocopying or other reprographic copying of any
part of this book must be directed in writing to Access Copyright: The Canadian
Copyright Licensing Agency, One Yonge Street, Suite 800, Toronto, Ontario,
Canada, M5E 1E5.

Anvil Press Publishers Inc.
P.O. Box 3008, Main Post Office
Vancouver, B.C. V6B 3X5 CANADA
www.anvilpress.com

Library and Archives Canada Cataloguing in Publication

Title: Borderline / by Marie-Sissi Labrèche ; translation by Melissa Bull.
Other titles: Borderline. English
Names: Labrèche, Marie-Sissi, 1969- author. | Bull, Melissa, 1977- translator.
Description: Translation of French book with same title.
Identifiers: Canadiana 20200186094 | ISBN 9781772141436 (softcover)
Classification: LCC PS8573.A246 B6713 2020 | DDC C843/.6—dc23

Cover design by Rayola.com
Interior by HeimatHouse
Represented in Canada by Publishers Group Canada
Distributed by Raincoast Books

The publisher gratefully acknowledges the financial assistance of the Canada
Council for the Arts, the Canada Book Fund, and the Province of British Columbia
through the B.C. Arts Council and the Book Publishing Tax Credit.

We acknowledge the financial support of the Government of Canada through the
National Translation Program for Book Publishing for our translation activities.

PRINTED AND BOUND IN CANADA

For André Carpentier.
And for my grandmother, Marie-Anne Naud.

Prologue

My grandmother's talked crap for as long as I can re-member. All kinds of crap. Like, if I was being bratty, she'd say: *If you aren't good, a faggot will climb through the window and rape you. Or, I'll sell you to the white slave trade. Or, A murderer will chop you into tiny pieces with a scalpel, is that what you want? Eh?* At four years old, I wasn't allowed the bogeyman or the *Bonhomme Sept-Heures*.[1] I got serial killers.

Yeah...she told me all kinds of crap that totally fucked with my mind and made me feel dumb as shit. That's why I'm scared of everything now: people; public spaces; cramped spaces; cows—because they're so big (don't get me started on whales); going out after 9 p.m. by myself; spiders and their long legs; centipedes and their hundreds of legs; high heels over inclined surfaces; incompetent shrinks; overly competent shrinks; public or private transportation; moving house; homeless people walking around with their bleeding scabs; punks with their squeegees jumping all over you to scrub you even if you don't have a windshield; foreigners who open dépanneurs[2] and can't understand you just want matches; smashing sounds; floors that creak at night; forms to fill out; bills to pay; the government with its octopus tentacles; hard drugs that make you hallucinate *Planet of the Apes* on every TV channel at the same time;

half-cooked, still-bleeding hamburger meat; Shirriff mashed potatoes; ghosts without white sheets; wrong numbers; butt-ugly rapists; butt-ugly killers; butt-ugly aunties who are actually terrorists; aneurisms exploding in your brain without warning; Pac-Man-like, starving streptococci; and AIDS—any fucking disease. But more than anything, what I'm most scared of is not being loved. So I spread my legs to get a little glimpse of heaven. I spread my legs to forget who I am. I spread my legs to shine like a little star. I love myself so little, I'll spread my legs for anyone who seems to like me even a tiny bit.

Chapter 1:

Cinderella

*Open up my legs / I will see the sky / Floating in this
space / Floating in this room / This hospital is cold / I
deceive everyone / But my salvation is close.*
— Sylph, "Charlatan"

Sherbrooke Street. I'm lying on a bed in a room at the
Château de l'Argoat. I'm lying very straight on my
back. Like a corpse in a coffin, my hands flat under my
breasts. If it wasn't for my legs, I'd definitely look like a
corpse in a coffin. My legs are wide open. My legs are
spread so wide they're almost on either side of my ears. I
just got fucked.

I could bring my two wide-open legs back together to
hide my cleft, but I don't. I don't know why. I don't know
anything. I don't even know what room number I'm in. I
had my head down when we came in. I was so ashamed, I
couldn't lift my eyes from the floor. The guy at the front
desk seemed like he knew too much about what we were
going to do all night. He knew we weren't going to play
Monopoly, that we were going do a ton of dirty things, and
it disgusted me. It disgusted me especially because I was
with Éric. Éric is super gross, super fat, super misshapen,
and super short. From behind his desk, the guy at the

BORDERLINE | 9

front must have imagined all the horrors of my night with Éric. Éric's huge tongue inside my little mouth, his fat, sticky paws fiddling with the tips of my sensitive breasts, his big belly on my teensy ass when he went inside me.

The guy at the front desk must have told himself: *It doesn't make sense! Not that beautiful blonde with... that ... that thing?!! She must be an escort! She must be doing it for money!*

I wanted to yell at him: *Yeah, I'm a whore! But not the kind of whore you think. I'm not a whore like on TV shows or on the corner of Champlain Street! I'm not fucking doing this for cash! I'm doing this to calm my fucking nerves! But you don't get it because you're no better than the fat guy who's about to fuck me in a couple of minutes. You're no better. Given the chance, you'd fuck me like crazy, too, even if you're as dull as a plate of shepherd's pie! You'd try to stick it everywhere, up to my ears if you could, you disgusting sodomizer.*

That's what I wanted to yell at him, at the guy at the front desk, that and a lot of other crap, but I shut it, as usual, and I didn't say anything. It's better if I shut it, anyway, because when I speak, I say only vile things, vile things that hurt everyone around me, like the vile things I said that worried my mother so much... How many times has my grandmother told me that? *You're good at talking crap. You're fucking great at talking crap that worries your mother.* Yeah, I'm fucking great at it!

I'm lying on the bed in this sad hotel room and I'm

crying. I'm crying like a moron, crying to the point of making my eyeballs pop out of my head. My tears shoot out like machine gun bullets, it's like I want to pierce all of humanity with my pain. I wet everything, I stain everything, too. My cheap mascara smears on my face, draws funny shapes over my skin, funny shapes that spread the storm inside my head across my cheeks. Because there's a storm inside my head. That's right. A big storm, with wind, rain, and even hurricanes. As soon as I close my eyes, it's El Niño behind my eyelids. It's El Niño with its millions of dollars' worth of damage, its thousands of dead, and countless devastated territories. I'm ashamed of myself. I'm so ashamed I could die. I don't know why I agreed to come here and fuck a guy I don't even like. I don't know why. Well, yes. I do. A little. His eyes shine really brightly when he looks at me . . . and he's been chasing me for so many years. I told myself, *Hey! What have you got to lose by fucking him? You've thrown yourself at uglier guys than him! Yeah, guys way more ugly than this guy.* And when he looks at me with his eyes rolling like marbles, it makes me feel needed. Anyway, as soon as a man looks at me with fried-cod eyes, I feel needed and I spread my legs. It's become a reflex, the way the Rorschach test was for my mother. My mother was crazy. A real crazy person with glazed eyes, unstable behaviour, and a thousand pills to take every day. A real crazy person with a real medical certificate, who often had

BORDERLINE | 11

to take the Rorschach test, so often that at the sight of a stain she couldn't help but say what it reminded her of: *A tulip! An elephant! A cloud! A disemboweled uterus! Chinese people eating rice!*

So when Éric looked at me with his fried-cod eyes I decided that, for one night, I would be his Cinderella. With my most beautiful dress on, I played the fairy. He could have his magical life for one night. I had the Disney-fying power to transform him from a frog into a Prince Charming. I sat, in my most beautiful dress, in the centre of the room, on an old wooden chair. I took off my under-wear and spread my legs, like Sharon Stone in *Basic Instinct*. I'd wanted to try that for a long time! Well! It didn't go unnoticed. Éric was just like the little fatty in the movie. Stereotypes must be genetic! His eyes got so wide, it was like they'd been treated by Softimage.[3] It was like being in the middle of a Molson Dry commercial, when people think they've discovered the musical capsule. Oh my god! I always want eyes like that. Always. It's my elixir. It's what I run on.

A little calculated shake of the shoulder and my thin silk strap dropped, uncovering my breast. Éric couldn't help himself. He bounded towards me like an acrobat from Cirque du Soleil, but without a trapeze or a hoop.

"Stay where you are, Éric, don't move."

No, he couldn't move, not right away, he had to stay there, looking at me, for as long as possible. He had to let his eyes shine on me, his eyes that made me more beautiful and made me forget that he was fat and lousy, and that I was messed up. Still spread open, in my head and on the bed.

"Oh Sissi! Sissi! You're so pretty! Oh! Oh! Oh! And your skin is so white! Oh! Oh! Oh!"

"Stop your 'Oh! Oh! Ohs!' You sound like Santa Claus. Stop doing that 'Oh! Oh! Oh!' stuff, Éric, and listen to me. You're going to do what I tell you to do. Every single thing. Okay?"

"Okay."

"I want you to lie down and just look at me."

I got up and put a cassette in the tape player I always carry with me. I can't stand myself without music, so I live my life to a filigreed soundtrack. A different soundtrack for every place, every person. I picked the soundtrack for the difficult task at hand: industrial. Striptease to the music of Ministry. Not bad! I've got to say that I was starting to get really fucking lit! His eyes and the booze. We were pretty much pickled. Dépanneur shit, but it still gets you drunk. It makes you see everything in Fujicolor, it could make a chair rail interesting. I'd downed at least three glasses of red, shot after shot. *Hurry up*, I told myself, now sitting on him, *you have to numb yourself, old girl*. And one, two, three, it was done. Alcohol acted on me like ether at the dentist. Except I wasn't getting a tooth pulled. But it was almost as bad.

BORDERLINE | 13

Why am I doing this? I asked myself as I wiggled my hips against him. *Why did I get myself into this? Like all the other times, with all the others? Fuck, I'm dumb. Fuck, I'm stupid. Fuck! Fuck! Fuck!*

A glass of wine in one hand, then quick, it's downed. My dress balled up over my thighs. My arms tumbled through the air, stopped at his sweater, which I lifted, and I rubbed my breasts against his enormous, covered-in-stretch-marks stomach. Gross! Quick, quick, another glass of wine. There. I was knocked out for good. I began to feel good and find him attractive.

That's when Éric started up in earnest and that's when I wanted to kill him. As soon as a man takes control, I want to kill him, to stick a big breadknife into his stomach and make zigzags. I asked myself if a fat guy would bleed more, if it would be harder to do it because of the layers of fat or if he would deflate and fly off in all directions like a balloon in the air. *Psssssssssoooooouuuuuuuuuuuuuuuu!* It made me laugh to imagine Éric deflating, flying left and right around the room, but I soon stopped. He was taking off what remained of my dress. I closed my eyes and let him touch me.

He was gentle with me. Very gentle. His hands were like cotton batten on my skin. He barely touched me, preferring to skim my skin. He was scared of missing his shot, you could feel it, so he was being as sweet as he could. I like it when they're careful. It makes it seem like they respect me, like they're scared of startling me, like I might bolt off to another country, another galaxy. I like to think that people care about me. I always thought my mother didn't care about me. I thought, because she so often escaped someplace in her head that I couldn't access, that she didn't care about me. My mother could spend weeks like that, in her head, staring at me, her expressionless blue eyes aimed in my direction, her eyes filled with a sadness that made me sick. Weeks like that, sitting in her rocking chair without rocking, staring at me. Without speaking. Not a word. Silent. Only the sound of the refrigerator, the sound of the upstairs neighbour's boiler, the sound of cockroaches scrabbling over my drawings strewn throughout the kitchen. But no comforting, reassuring words came out of her mouth. None. And, sitting on the floor, at her feet, I told her stories with the help of my dolls and my little Fisher-Price figurines; stories she didn't even understand because of her goddamned defective hormones, her goddamned expired hormones.

Gently, Éric put his lips on the tip of my breast and began to lick it. I felt nothing. It bored me. I wasn't making any sounds, so I thought he would get it and hurry up a little. But no! He persisted with his gentleness. Again, a too-soft lick, and another, and another. Always too soft. I don't like when I have to open my mouth to tell them what to do. I don't know much about how couples communicate. The only role models I had were my mother and my stepfather, and they can be summed up in two sentences: *Fuck off, you big, damn dirty dog! Eat shit, crazy lady!* What am I saying? That's not even true. I just made that up. I talk crap all the time, fuck. It wasn't even my stepfather who spoke like that to my mother! No! My stepfather just talked to the wall because he felt more understood. And my mother didn't talk back like that to my stepfather, either. My mother was the gentlest person in the world! All the world's gentleness was concentrated into a bacteriological bomb on the point of exploding in the face of the first person to show up, which would be me. So then I appeared, and bang! The bomb exploded in my face. There you go! Your own fault for being there when you shouldn't have been, you curious little kid. You just couldn't mind your own beeswax, you little good-for-nothing. Now I'm infected, and I'll be stuck dragging my mother in my cells for centuries and centuries.

Éric kept licking me too softly. And that was it, I was seriously annoyed, seriously pissed.

"Please suck harder, Éric."

Finally. He sucked harder, except my pleasure was half-ruined because I'd opened my mouth and hearing the sound of my Barbie voice made me realize I was there, in a sad hotel room, with a short, fat, super ugly guy who was getting ready to get to work on me. Quick, some wine, quick! As I was about to drink, Éric took the glass and poured its contents down my body. I thought of the waste.

Thousands of people are starving to death in Bangladesh. Then he started to lap up the liquid. Not so original. It's been seen in a ton of movies, except it's still exciting, especially when a little dimpled finger rolls inside me at the same time. I closed my eyes. It was actually good. Almost as good as the time my prof did it to me in an empty classroom at the Cégep[4] du Vieux Montréal.

My head turned. Left, right, right, left, left, right, right, left. I was totally drunk, finally, and I was feeling good about myself, but it didn't last. Éric started to penetrate me. A big thing trying to go into my belly. My vagina started to have stupid contractions. It always does that when I'm surprised. Éric had a hard time getting inside me because of his enormous stomach and the contractions, so with a sudden move, he flipped me over. I didn't think he was controlling his desire very well. I found myself on all fours, and then, with a big shove, he went in, in one shot, all the way inside me. A cry. *AAAAAHHHHHH!* It burned. I thought everything had ripped. Despite my cries he started to let himself go. Forward and back, forward, back, forward, back, forward, picking up speed. He was deaf with desire. A plane could have landed in the room and he wouldn't have heard it. It had been years since he'd had sex, so he did the deed with vim and vigour. He made so many waves, it felt like being fucked by a waterbed! And the sound, too. Bloop! Bloop! Bloop! I liked it even if it burned, because his dick was enormous, as big as an ocean liner. It felt like I was being filled, as lived in as a two-and-a-half[5] no longer alone in my cave. For a few minutes, the hollowness of my twenty-three years of existence evaporated, erased. No more filth-filled emptiness. No crazy mother, no fear, no nagging grandmother, no worries. Just me and a dick. But all good things come to an end. Éric started to make weird noises. The waterbed turned into a caveman. *HUM! HUM! HUM!* He pulled out and came on me. All over my back. I even got some in my hair. I hate that. I looked like a colander dripping spaghetti.

"I'm sorry I couldn't hold back anymore. I'm sorry, I know that...you know...it wasn't very long that...I hadn't done that," he said, all ashamed.

"Don't worry. It's fine."

A kiss on the forehead and quickly to sleep.

"You didn't kiss me once, Sissi."

So. This again.

"But I just gave you a big kiss on the forehead."

"No, I mean a kiss on the mouth...with tongue."

"I have bad breath, you know...I just drank all that booze..."

"I want you to kiss me. You don't like me? Is that it? Come on...kiss me."

He was starting to act like a rutting walrus cooing like a pigeon in springtime. The fat ones, the too-skinny ones, the ugly ones, you give them an inch and they take a mile. They crave affection so badly that when they get someone, they drain them in two seconds flat. But now the lemon had lost its juice, it was just citric acid. And if he didn't quit toying with my goodwill, I was going to pour all my gall in his face. It wouldn't be pretty—I'd been holding back a long time.

I gave him my worst look and that must have been something. But it didn't seem to bother him because he started up again. "Kiss me..." he said. "Kiss me on the mouth..." offering up the little slit that was supposed to be his mouth. He disgusted me. On top of having breasts as large as mine, he didn't have a mouth. It was eaten up by his enormous face, his face made entirely of cheeks. I hated him. I wanted to kill him even more.

I don't know how I did it, but I closed my eyes and I kissed him. All along, I thought of the knife in my bag. Would I stab him? Would I stab myself? Should I stab everything in the room?

I felt a hand between my legs. Oh, no! Not again. I had to think of something so he'd get away from there and give me a bit of breathing space. I had to be alone or I'd start breaking things.

"Éric, please, later. I'm starving. Why don't you get us something to eat? What do you think?"

He couldn't refuse. He's fat for a reason—he eats all the time. He eats more than his own emotions. He eats all the emotions of the Earth from the beginning of time. He eats emotion pies, emotion canapés, emotion cakes, emotion pâtés, turkeys stuffed with feelings…

"Come on, say yes. I feel like I could eat some lasagna. Wouldn't some lasagna be good?"

"Yes, you're right. I'll go. But don't move. Okay? Promise?"

"I won't move."

He got up and got dressed in front of me. Slowly, casually. He was a little too comfortable for my liking. For a moment he even started to imitate a stripper, but a stripper in rewind, as he put his clothes back on. Wagging his butt in my face, he threw coquettish glances out of the corners of his eyes, mischievous little smiles. I watched him, all along, and smiled as if I found it charming, as if I was saying, *Oh Éric, you're amazing! You're so this! You're so that! You're so the man of my dreams! Where would I be without you?* I affected my most candid expression, the expression that could make anyone believe I was sincere, a kind of limpid face, transparent, with very big and brilliantly shining eyes, a beatific smile, the whole thing framed with my hair drawn back behind my ears like Dopey in *Snow White and the Seven Dwarves*.

Poor Éric. If only he could guess how much I hated him at that moment. I hated him to the point of no return, to the point of forgetting he was a human being. I hated him like crazy, with his big, soft belly and his big, stupid smile. I wanted to tie him up so I could cut off his dick and balls and stuff the whole package up his ass, rip out his eyes and make him eat them without salt or pepper, lacerate his big belly, dig some more stretch marks into it, jam fries up his nose and stop his mouth with a dirty, old sock to watch him choke, go blue, see his eyes spin back, his soft body go even softer and spread out on the chair like Cheez Whiz on toast. If he could have guessed how much I hated him, he would have run away at top speed, super far away.

"I'll be back. It won't take me long. You'll wait?"

"Of course, Éric. Of course."

It must be a good ten minutes since he left. I've had time to think all sorts of super negative things and to cry all the tears out of my body. I'm ready, now. I'm going to leave. I will eclipse myself from Éric's life. From his life and from the lives of all the friends we have in common. I've slept with all his friends, anyway, making each of them promise to keep it a secret. But I know very well Éric won't be able to keep it a secret. Nothing ever happens to him and he loves me so much he'll be too eager to share his happiness with the whole world. I can already imagine it: *Hey, guys, you won't believe what happened to me! You won't! I made love with the woman of my dreams! Who? Who? Who? Sissi. No! Yes!!! No! Yes!!!*

Uh, me too, Gabriel will say. *Me too,* Dany will say. *Me too,* Bernard will say. *Me too,* René will say. *Me too,* Tristan will say. *Me too*, Daniel will say. *Me too*, André will say. *Me too*, Tony will say. *Me too*, Jérôme will say. *Me too*, Sacha will say. *Me too*, Isabelle will say. And then they'll all start talking about me, like group therapy about their lives with Sissi, their feelings about Sissi, their nights with Sissi, their orgasms with Sissi. It'll never end. I'm dead meat!

I have to get out, there's nothing left for me with them … They'll see I'm a charlatan. A charlatan in a carnival, a charlatan in a masquerade, a charlatan who makes herself out to be Cinderella and thinks of gifting people with magic nights with the wands of others. Here, Éric, I'll leave you my panties instead of a glass slipper. You can keep them as a souvenir. You won't have a choice. You can ask all the women on Earth to try them on, they won't fit any of them. They belonged to my ex-boyfriend.

Chapter 2:

The Invention of Death

Chateaugué is dead. The poor idiot, the poor nut killed
herself. If she killed herself to soften me to her, she
missed her shot. I don't care! [...] I kind of want to
laugh. I'm as tired as a fucking comic.

— Réjean Ducharme, *Le nez qui voque*[6]

I'm eleven years old and watching *Les tannants*[7] on TV.
Roger Giguère[8] is dressed like a buffoon and he's hitting
Shirley Théroux[9] on the butt with a stick. I see the images
but I can't understand anything. I'm having a hard time
concentrating. It's like there's a ball in my throat. A ball
that's growing so much it's turning into a watermelon.
Everything is muddled, I don't know if I want to cry or
vomit. I'm swimming in a dream. When I turn from the
television and look around at the rooms of our house,
everything starts to move, it's like watching life through
a kaleidoscope. So for now, I'd rather stare at the TV, waiting. Waiting for what? I don't know. My mother just committed suicide. She took some lithium, some Luvox, some
Dalmane, and some Valium; she took all her pills at the
same time. Then she yelled: *I LOVE YOU ALL!*

Funny way of loving people.

For a while, there was a lot of commotion in the apartment. Everyone was freaking out. My mother screamed, my stepfather cried, and the people on TV yelled because Pierre Marcotte[10] announced the winner of the Elvis impersonator contest. I just wanted to know who'd won; I'd been following the competition for weeks. But my mother decided to throw away her life and everyone else's right then. My mother kept me from watching TV all day. My mother is the stick in my bicycle spokes. She always chooses the perfect moment to stage her crap. My mother's just like that. She always has to have all the attention on her, she has to be the focal point. The worst part is, it always works, even with me. My mother is my target. I use her to work out my bugs. I throw my cockroaches at her, my mosquitoes on her, my spiders on her. My mother is my Montreal Insectarium. I cover her with vermin so I won't see what I could look like, later. I don't want to be like her. I fight it. Everything she likes I don't like. Everything she's done I don't do. I don't want to be her. *Nyet. Non.* No. I am not her.

"Quick, Sissi! Do something!" says my stepfather through his tears. "I can't stay, your grandmother will say I'm the one who forced her to take all her pills."

My grandmother never misses the chance to accuse my stepfather of something. He's her punching bag. Her scapegoat. Her spittoon. She throws all sorts of things at his head: water glasses, bottles of Quik, jam jars, sticks, stones, anything goes. He's her favourite target. To each their own! She even sleeps with a brick beside her bed. She told me if ever he tried to get into her room, she'd be ready with a brick and a flashlight. I never found the flashlight.

I called the emergency at Notre-Dame Hospital. I don't know how I did it. I don't remember anything. In fact, I think another little girl did it for me. A little blonde girl like me, who smiled and took my hand to dial the number. She spoke, too. "Hello, is this the Notre-Dame Hospital? Good. I'd like an ambulance, it's my mother. She's gone and done her imitation of Marilyn Monroe. It was very well done. We all applauded. But now she doesn't want to get off the stage. So quick, send us an ambulance or a camera crew, because I'd like to get back to watching television. I want to know who won the Elvis competition." Then, the little girl told me: "Come on, let's go see who won." So the little girl and I watched TV.

I heard the door open and close. Several men came in. The police showed up, and detectives, paramedics, doctors. I don't think there'd ever been as many people in the house. It was like Christmas at my uncle Michel's. But it wasn't a fun celebration because no one was smiling, everyone looked like disaster victims, it was a disaster celebration. I didn't go look in the room where my mother was. No. I stayed in front of the TV watching *Les tannants*. A police officer came to see me. He spoke some words to me, but I couldn't understand them. He put his hand on my hair and

BORDERLINE | 25

smiled. I just saw his teeth. He had a broken tooth at the front of his mouth. I wanted to make myself very small, to crawl inside his mouth and set myself on his tongue so he could swallow me.

A voice spoke: *Her uncle can look after her.*

It was my grandmother's voice. How did she get here? As far as I knew, she was running errands all day. It took hours to run so many errands. My grandmother is like God. She is manifest everywhere. Or I should say feminist everywhere, because she crushes everything male to a pulp. She says that men are assholes who think only of themselves: they beat women, drink like fish, make babies all over the place, and gamble away their paycheques. I'll contradict my grandmother when I'm older. I'll marry all the men on Earth just to piss her off. She's pissed me off enough with the Raisin Bran she makes me eat every morning. "Eat up, it'll keep you regular," she says all the time. The world is upside down, everything is backwards, inside out, but I poop every day at the same time. What good does it do me?

In under two minutes, the whole house empties itself like when you flush the water in the toilet bowl. My mother is on a stretcher, and everyone leaves with her, the focal point. They leave me there, all alone. I don't know who won the Elvis competition. I don't know if my mother died. I don't know what will happen to me. The television is off. I turned it off. It's quiet. There's no more

26 | BORDERLINE

noise in the house, just the grumblings of my stomach. I'm hungry, but I can't eat. There isn't anyone around to make me any food, and in any case my stomach is already too full. The emptiness fills me. It flies into each of my cells at a vertiginous speed; it's faster than the Millennium Falcon in *Star Wars*. I lie down on the living room floor. The ground is cold, my back is freezing. I don't care. I won't get up. I don't ever want to move. The emptiness is so heavy.

❋ ❋ ❋

I wake up in my bed. My grandmother or my uncle must have put me there. I can't remember anything. My brain is applesauce. I feel like I was pummelled all night. I woke up because of the sound of pots clanging against each other. My grandmother does the dishes so loudly. She washes the dishes like a goddamned fanatic.

I had nightmares all night. Gangsters disguised as Elvis Presley pursued me, but I was frozen on the spot. Paralyzed. Legs like concrete. Brain full of lightning. Vocal cords knotted. But as soon as I opened my eyes, happy to finally be free of the goddamned dreams, reality was waiting for me with its firm, anxious grip. Images from the night before came to me all of a sudden: my mother naked, robe open, yelling, "I LOVE YOU ALL"; my stepfather crying; the policeman with the broken tooth; the empty pill bottles on the dirty kitchen table. IS MY MOTHER DEAD OR WHAT?

Quick, head to the kitchen.

"Mémé! Mémé! Did Môman die?"

My grandmother doesn't look away from the dirty dishes. She's silent a long time. I watch while three cockroaches thread along the old percolator they live in; it's their housing project. My grandmother never answers me right away. She lets me languish. So I show her I can languish. In a white undershirt, bare feet on the frozen linoleum, I fucking languish. My skin turns blue, I look like Smurfette. I put one foot over the other to try to get warm as much as to keep the cockroaches on the floor from touching me.

Finally, my grandmother's eyes leave the dirty dishes and she opens her mouth. She breaks the news to me in a voice as dry as soda crackers.

"They don't know if they're going to get her back, but, right now, she's alive. Still. We'll know more tonight... None of this would have happened if your goddamned stepfather hadn't been there. He must've forced her to take all those pills. He wants to kill her. I know it. He's an assassin! He's a goddamned dog! A goddamned dog!"

"He's not, Mémé... stop. It's not his fault. You know what your daughter says..."

"Oh, you're just like your stepfather. You're always taking his side. You too... Wouldn't you like it if your

28 | BORDERLINE

mother died. But I'll tell you...if she dies, I might have to put you in foster care, and I've told you about what happens in those families—it's not good. Anyway, don't ask me any more questions. Eat your Raisin Bran, it's good for you." I go to my corner with my bowl of Raisin Bran. My cereal's turning to mush. My grandmother must have put the bowl on the table a half hour ago. The cereal is completely soaked in milk. It looks like floating black chunks are trying to escape the brown purée. My cereal is as sad as me. Still, I keep the bowl in my hands. It keeps me busy. I don't want to fight with my grandmother this morning. I don't want to fight with her ever. I'm sick of it. I'm sick of watching her get mad, because when she gets mad, she always takes it out on me, and I take it right in the face. She tells me I'm nasty, that I only think of hurting other people, that I'm corrupt, and that one day she'll put me in foster care. But I don't mind. She can say all the crap she wants all year long if she wants. Put me in foster care! She's been singing that old tune for a thousand years. *If you're not good, I'll put you in foster care. If you don't finish your dinner, I'll put you in foster care. If you tell a lie, I'll put you in foster care. If you pick your nose, I'll put you in foster care! If you move the juice box, I'll put you in foster care! I'll put you in care! I'll put you in care! I'm going to put you in foster care like it's no one's business! I'm going to put you in foster care on another planet!* There! Pluto's the farthest! Like she'd really do it. She just wants me to scare

BORDERLINE | 29

me, the meanie. She's sick to her old, rotted bones with ill will, and she wants me to be as wrecked with worry as she is.

Céline picks me up on her way to school the way she does every morning. Céline, my Raisin Bran friend. My gauge of regularity in all the chaos. Rain or shine, Céline is on the job, always at the ready. This morning, Céline's acting sweet. Not because my mother committed suicide. No, she doesn't know that yet. Because we fought, yesterday, right before *Les tannants*. Come to think of it, yesterday was really a big day. A big, sad, broom closet of a day. A big-ass day of crap! Céline didn't want to play bingo with me, and I slapped her. She ran home crying. And still this morning she shows up. Céline doesn't have any self-respect. She's got poodle loyalty running in her veins.

"I'm sorry about yesterday," she says to me. "We're friends...okay?"

I'm the one who hit her and she's the one saying sorry. Goddamned Céline!

"Okay, Céline, but next time, listen to me. If I say we're playing bingo, we're playing bingo!"

I can always find an excuse to teach her a lesson, my lesson. Poor Céline. I pity her. She needs me so much, like a can of peas needs a can opener. I'm the one who defends her at school. She always puts her foot in her mouth because she's slow in the head. But anyway. It works for me, I feel needed. And plus, this morning, I'm particularly happy she's here. I couldn't wait to tell someone that my mother committed suicide. An event like that gives me importance; it makes me the focal point.

I take on a tragic air to announce the news to Céline. It feels like I'm living in a movie. What's happening is such a big deal, I have to force myself to look like I'm really into it. When these things happen to me, I divide myself in two; one part is pretending, while the other hides and trembles.

"Céline, my mother took all her pills to kill herself yesterday."

"Is she dead?"

"Not yet. We'll know more tonight."

"Wow! What are you going to do?"

"Oh, I don't know... Maybe my grandmother will put me in foster care to live with another family."

"Oh, no! Poor you."

"Do you know what will probably happen to me if she puts me in foster care?"

"No, what will happen to you?"

"My grandmother told me that if I get a good family then that would be okay, and I'd have lots of nice dresses. I'd go to school in a limousine and I'd have all the Barbies in the world. But, if I get a bunch of jerks who adopt kids just for the money, they'll only feed me toast without any butter. And I'll wear the other kids' old clothes, all second-hand, full of holes. And they'll only let me wash myself with cold water and no soap. Also maybe the daddy will want to play his funny game with me."

"Play a funny game with you?"

"Yeah, you know, he'll show me his thing…his dick."

"Oh! His dick!"

"He'll want me to put it in my mouth, all the way inside my little mouth. And this big, gross guy will stick it so far down my throat, he'll suffocate me. And I won't be able to run away because he'll grip my head with his two, gross, dirty hands with dirty nails. The lights will be out, so he won't be able to tell I'm turning blue, that I'm dying."

"No! That's horrible. I don't want that to happen to you! Do something…"

"Yeah, I'll do something, I'll bite his big dick."

"Yeah, until it bleeds!"

"I'll even tear it off. And you know what I'll do with it?"

"No!"

"I'll chew it, in front of him, like this, CRUNCH, CRUNCH, CRUNCH! And I'll chomp on his dick until it's hamburger meat. And then, for sure, technology won't be able to do anything for him. He won't be able to sew it back on."

"That'll serve him right, the gross, dirty dog!"

"Then I'll run away and hide in the woods. I'll build a house with branches. You'll be the only one who'll know where I live. That way you can bring me McDonald's and my homework."

"Your homework?"

"Well, yeah! Because I'll have to study by myself. I won't be able to go to school. Because the cops will be after me because I'll have mutilated the foster family father. But I won't go to a reform school. My grandmother said it's terrible what happens there, it's worse than in foster families! The security guards gang up twenty at a time to make the little girls pass the test."

"What test?"

"It's a resistance test. They stick everything they can find in the little girls' stomachs. They put crayons, beer bottles, clubs. Anything they can get their hands on. If you resist, if you pass the test, they leave you alone and you become the property of some of them, but just while you're there. But if you don't resist, your stomach explodes, and all the objects come out of your belly button."

"Stop! It's too awful. Stop! You're my only friend. I don't want anything bad to happen to you. No. You should come and live with me instead. I'll hide you in my room and we'll always sleep together."

That's it, Céline is crying. She's as worried about me as I am. I'm thrilled. I feel less alone in my crap. I apply my grandmother's principle: a sorrow shared is a sorrow halved. I'm like Mémé. I'm strong. I don't cry. I haven't cried. I'll save that for later. When I'm lying on a bed in a shitty hotel room after getting fucked by a fatso. For now, like my grandmother, I don't cry, and, like her, I can also

BORDERLINE | 33

wash dishes like a fucking fiend, to make all my veins, all the arteries in my body explode, to spew myself against the kitchen's yellow walls and into both my mothers' eyes. I'm bottling it up for the future. One day, it'll be my moment of glory!

Chapter 3:

Creep

I want to have control / I want a perfect body / I want a perfect soul / I want you to notice / When I'm not around / You're so fucking special / I wish I was special / But I'm a creep / I'm a weirdo / What the hell am I doing here? / I don't belong here.

— Radiohead, "Creep"

It's my birthday today. Twenty-four years old. Happy birffffffffffffday to meeeeeeeeee! But I so don't give a shit! I could be forty for all I care. I could be Queen Victoria for all I care. I don't care the way I don't care if it's butter or margarine. Some say it's healthier to eat butter, others say the opposite. Margarine, butter, I don't care. I eat poutine with McCain fries, McDonald's almost every day, and tons of candy. I'll get intestinal cancer and die. Fuck intestines! Hail solitude!

I'm at a big loft my friends have had the kindness to rent to celebrate my birthday. They're all having fun like I'm not here. I'm in a corner, all alone, sitting against a wall. My legs folded in front of me. I hold them tightly with my arms. The red, yellow, green, and blue lights twinkle against my skin. I don't have any tights on even though it's November, the month of my birthday, the month of the dead.

BORDERLINE | 35

I'm all alone in a crowd of so-called friends who came to wish me happy birthday, who came to shake a paw. Fuck you! Paws off! I'm just talking out of my ass. I drank like a good girl. I drank a lot. I drank enough to knock out my bladder.

Red wine, not blood, flows through my veins. I'm totally trashed. People come over to say happy birthday and I laugh in their faces. I make fun of them. I laugh at them. I laugh in their faces. A courageous few come over to tell me I'm pretty, they like the way I'm dressed, I'm cool...But that just has the butter-or-margarine effect on me: I don't care. I don't care about anything. Earlier, I danced and slammed against the loft wall. There's no more wall, now. It's not my fault if the walls are made of cardboard. The owner will probably take me to court, but I don't care about that, either. I don't have any money.

It's my birthday today and I'm singing songs in my head. I sing in my head because my voice sounds like a radio stuck between stations. I've smoked too many cigarettes today. I know because I blew out every match carefully, as if I was blowing out the candles on my birthday cake. It's my birthday but no one thought of buying me a birthday cake. My friends suck at birthdays! They never get it right. My mother wouldn't have forgotten. She would have bought me a nice cake with white icing and blue flowers, or a cake with a Barbie in the middle. My mother didn't forget cakes. Even from her solitary confinement at the hospital, she didn't forget cakes. She called and cried for hours on the phone because she couldn't bring me one. But my supposed friends have forgotten. So it won't be a real birthday for me. Whatever! I don't care, anyway!

The lights keep reflecting on my legs, my thighs. It's pretty. I'm getting really fucking excited! I lift my skirt a little. The lights follow me. I'm not wearing any underwear. Everyone can see my blonde pussy, but I don't care about that, either. In fact, I'd like it if someone saw me and came over to look at the little birthday lights shimmering on my legs and thighs. If they came over, I think I'd let them look at the lights on my thighs, my stomach, my breasts... that would cheer me up... but no one comes over. I drank too much and I'm scaring them, but at least they stay at the party. They stay because the beer is free, the beer and the wine. But there isn't any more wine. I drank it all. If they want more, they'll have to open my veins. They'll just have to suck my blood; the whole gang will have to get on top of me and suck me, suck me. They've always sucked my energy; they'd be capable of it.

It's my birthday and I want to get fucked.

I set myself a challenge. If no one comes over in the next five minutes, I'll go over to them and it won't be pretty. I'll make a scene! I'll cause a ruckus! I'll get noticed! Come on. Do they really think I'm going to let them drink all my birthday booze without someone coming over to check out the lights on my stomach and thighs? My patience has its limits, and so do my clothes. If they don't come and look at me soon, I'm going to do something big. I'll put on a show. *Come on in, come on in, come see the show, you can even bring your women and children, it will be educational!* I'll make a spectacle of myself. I'll make an Annie Sprinkle of myself! The first brave soul who dares approach me can have me to themselves for the night. What a deal! No need to flirt, no need to tell me I'm pretty, I'm nice, none of that. No. It'll be instant, like the coffee, like Maxwell House. But I know them. None of them will come to see me and fewer would even stop me...Stop me. Well. If only. They'll stop me but not before seeing how far I'll go, how deeply I can sink myself into my barrel. At first, they'll act like they're shocked at my behaviour. But they won't be able to stop watching me. Their inner strength, their inner stronghold will get an eyeful of my audacity. They'll be walled in behind their well-compartmentalized, well-controlled feelings. My feelings are impossible to hold back. They overflow, like puke out of a paper bag. That's why I control myself so badly. In fact, I can't control myself at all: I explode. I'm my own bomb. It's a permanent nuclear war in my brain, in my wake: cataclysms, catacombs, carnage. I'm my own worst-case scenario. Still worse is the fact that I found myself before I even started looking for myself. I found myself and now I can't get rid of myself. If I could, I'd borrow a life to rest in; to take a break from my own clinginess. It's

38 | BORDERLINE

disgusting how clingy I am. A real fly on shit. There's no way to get out of myself. To get out of this. What's going on? I don't have any more alcohol in my glass. Shit, I don't have anything left to drink! I have to go to the bar.

I try to get up but can't. My legs are like the sea, like a sea filled with sad fish. I give myself some momentum. There! The walls distend. It must be because of my salt water, erosion, and all of that. Quick, some wine! Quick, some beer! Quick, some tequila! Alcohol! Someone get me some alcohol!

A head leans towards me. Someone finally has the guts to come up to my little old self. But who is this Adonis who casts a shadow across my thighs? It's my ex-boyfriend and he's smiling at me. Right! The supreme ex-boyfriend. The ex-boyfriend to beat all ex-boyfriends.

"Happy birthday, Sissi!"

"Hey, Antoine, take me to your place. There's no more wine and I need to calm the alcoholic fish in my stomach..."

"I'd love to bring you home with me, sweetie, but I'm not sure my girlfriend would appreciate that. Anyway, you can't ditch your own birthday party, everyone's here for you..."

"I shouldn't even be here. I swore to myself I'd never see them again but they're always there, like stains. *And they call me: Sissi, come over here; Sissi, go over there...*"

"They love you, Sissi. Half of them are crazy about you. You could choose any of them..."

I stare at my ex-boyfriend, disconcerted, and start to

BORDERLINE | 39

laugh. I laugh a big, greasy laugh. I laugh with my throat unfurled. I laugh so loudly you can tell I'm not buying what he's saying. Choose anyone, choose anyone...he's funny, my ex-boyfriend, a real Michel Courtemanche[11] grin, a real *Surprise sur prise* by Marcel Béliveau.[12] Didn't my ex say to me, not that long ago: You see, when I'm not there, you always make the wrong choices? And what my mother always said was no better. *Eeny, meeny, miny, mo! Damned if you do, damned if you don't.* So when you talk to me about choice, I laugh my face off, I laugh my head off, I laugh for days, months, years, until I choke on my whole body. Choice. Choice. That's funny. He thinks I have a choice! Does he have choices? Of course he does! But not everyone gets to be the world's most kickass person. I'm the world's best piece of ass, and I've known for a long time who gets to choose and who doesn't. I let myself be had. I let myself go. I don't choose. I let myself be chosen, like a doll. But this doll is pretty much at the end of her rope. A little girl has scribbled on her face. She painted her teeth black, cut her hair very short, and ripped off her legs. So the doll can't make her way to the bar or get herself home.

"Antoine, can you take me home? I feel like a broken computer that's got to go back to the factory."

"Sure."

My ex-boyfriend puts his arm around my waist and holds me tight so I don't fall on the floor, like toast that falls on the jammy side. He's hurting me. His bones are hurting my bones. Every step creates electric eruptions that discharge in my brain. We're a couple of skeletons rubbing against each other. He drags me like he often did when I was drunk. In our wake, people disperse: the crowd opens like the sea at Moses' command. I would even add that people whisper and stare at us, if the Radiohead music weren't so loud. "BUT I'M A CREEP / I'M A WEIRDO / WHAT THE HELL AM I DOING HERE? / I DON'T BELONG HERE. / OH OH..." I'm a creep, too. A fucking creep, and I can't wait to get out of here. I'm cold, I'm hungry, everything hurts.

"Antoine, why did we break up?"

"We didn't break up...you ditched me for some poser artist, who you ditched for some shit photographer, who you ditched for..."

He doesn't stop. He reproaches me the whole way down the stairs. I would like to say maybe it's his fault I left him. It's true! It's not my fault he didn't take good care of me. He was as predictable as an American movie, all he cared about were his goddamn paintings. But it doesn't matter. Anyway, how could I fight with my ex when I've slept with half his friends?

"Okay, stop, Antoine. I get it."

"You shouldn't drink so much. You should focus on your studies, and you..."

The asshole goes on and on, and on top of everything

he starts dispensing life lessons. *You should take yourself in hand, you should... you should...* He's always preaching at me. He thinks he's my dad, or worse, my boss. Our relationship wasn't a real relationship, in fact, it was a start-up gone wrong, a start-up that went bankrupt because love and business don't mix.

"Fuck off, Antoine!"

"What?"

"I said, 'Fuck off, Antoine!'"

"Stop it, Sissi."

"Get out of here, go fuck yourself, or I'm going to punch you someplace."

"Stop it, you've had too much to drink."

"Go away! Go away! Go away!"

I start punching him. I try to aim for his torso but I just hit air. I look like an orchestra conductor conducting to empty chairs. And another punch to the wind, and another. But he's right next to me. What's happening? What's going on?

He doesn't know how to react while I'm doing this, he doesn't know where to look, doesn't know what to do. Good for him. He never knew what to do with me, anyway. I wasn't the girl for him. He needs a little dog to follow him everywhere, a little dog who loves his art, because for my ex, that's what love is. You have to admire him, idolize him, adore him, swear a sacred vow to him, because he supposedly paints nice paintings... Kill the calf, the chicken, and disembowel a young virgin on his altar, to pay homage to his alleged artistic talent. And why not slit the throats of every Tom, Dick, and Harry, while you're at it!

"ASSHOLE! I'M NOT THE GIRL FOR YOU!...AND YOUR PAINTINGS AREN'T EVEN ANY GOOD! GET AWAY!"

He doesn't react. I feel like I'm showing Avon products to a family of living dead. I want him to leave, I don't want to see his little go-getter face. I resent him. I resent him to death, but I don't know why, I can't remember why... He bothers me, that's why. Always lavishing advice on me. I don't need advice, just a nice, hard cock, ready for action. I want him to go. It's going to be every man for himself.

"YOU CAN'T FUCK! THAT'S WHY I BROKE UP WITH YOU! FUCK!"

That's bull. It's wrong. It's not a level playing field. I'm hitting below the belt, in our duel, because that particular region is my specialty. I am a castrator. A castrata. I make a song of my body to better cut off their family jewels with my sharp teeth. I hammer their skeletons to the bed to be sure I've got them in hand. Once I have them in my grip, I slip in two, three words. Just two, three telling words about their sexual potential, and there it goes! I ruin everything. It's funny, they're all afraid of me, but they all come back for more. I know why they come back. Because I'm good with their bodies. I'm good with their

BORDERLINE | 43

bodies, with my mouth, with my cleft. I'm a remake of *Emmanuelle*,[13] new and improved, harder and without any commercial breaks.

"I'M NOT THE KIND OF GIRL YOU NEED, ASSHOLE…"

I'm not anyone's type of girl. I'm not even a girl at all. I'm a case for the DSM-IV. I'm a case study, a specimen to dissect, like a mouse in a laboratory. In fact, the shrink at the CLSC[14] figured that out and wanted me to go get some help. Get some help! Help for what, exactly? To get labelled a nutcase, like my crazy mother? To be deemed not normal, like my not-normal mother? Or just be classified a good fuck? I just want to get fucked!

My ex-boyfriend leaves. Sad. I'm sad, too. Sad to have told him crap, crap that wasn't even true. Sad to have caused him pain, always causing more pain… sadness like I make for the whole world, like I do my mother… I'm in front of the loft's doorway, on the corner of Pins and Saint-Laurent. I can hear the shouts of happiness upstairs. Hey! Those are my birthday shouts. People are celebrating my birthday. People are drinking my birthday beer. I want to go back. I want to be the Queen of the Night.

Gripping the walls, I climb the staircase and go back into my birthday. The lights are still shining as brightly. I move painfully into the crowd. Fuck, my legs are heavy! It's like I'm dragging a ball and chain. It must be the weight of my guilt, guilt for having told my ex-boyfriend to piss off, guilt for being who I am, some kind of phony crap, guilty of existing, guilt, guilt...*L'arbre est dans ses feuilles Marilon Marilé!*[15] I walk, eyes fuzzy from the lights, lacerated by sidelong stares that are made my way. I approach my liberation. I'm getting closer. The others pretend not to see me. But they'll look at me and they won't have a choice, they won't be able to look away.

Once in the centre of the room, right in the middle, right under the pretty little red, yellow, green, and blue birthday lights, I start my act. I take off my black blazer slowly. I unbutton my black shirt slowly. I pull down my black skirt slowly. Slowly, I remove my red bra. I lie on the floor and I start to jerk off. The pointer finger of my right hand goes into my cleft and comes back out.

While the index finger of my left hand brushes the tip of my left breast, like in a porno, I can feel them, the others, they're starting to get edgy, and I can't help it, I burst out laughing.

I hear indignant cries from all over the place. *Oh, no! What is she doing? What's the matter with Sissi? Stop! No!* Hands touch me. Thousands of hands move over my body. They throw clothes at me, they pull one arm, then another. Someone takes advantage of the moment to touch my breasts. I knew they wouldn't be able to help themselves. Finally, people are taking care of me. Finally, I'm the Queen of the Night, and I feel a little better. I am tossed from side to side. The crowd rocks me like my mother used to, long ago, in a past life. I sway, I wade into the belly of the sea. It's calm under the waves. I feel good. It's quiet. Then it's nighttime. Where did all the little red, yellow, green, and blue lights go? Who stole my birthday lights? And who are all these Smurfs? Why are they moving so much? Hey! Do something! The Smurfs are going to kill me...

❀   ❀   ❀

I wake up in the middle of the night in the living room at my house, at my grandmother's house. I'm disoriented. I've lost my way. Someone left me here. I was cast here right in the middle of the living room where the light from the moon shines through the torn nylon curtains and mirrors millions of little stars across my skin. I'm sweating even though I'm as cold as a Popsicle. I try to get up but I fall. What's happening? My legs are asleep. So is my stomach. I feel sick. I feel so sick to my...

I vomit, completely naked, on all fours, right in the middle of the living room. I vomit wine and bile like a moron. My grandmother is there. She cleans up the mess, all the while muttering, "It doesn't make sense to drink like that! It doesn't make sense!" I want to tell her: Yes, Mémé, it makes sense to drink like this. It makes a lot of sense because wine flows through my veins, Mémé. Winter flows in my veins, Mémé. That's why my bones are snow, that's why

46 | BORDERLINE

I'm cold, why I have badly-kissed blue lips. My lips are as blue as Laura Palmer's. I emanate cold. I'm cold, Mémé. I can't warm up, anymore. All the bodies of the world can't warm me, anymore. No words can comfort me. Nothing is ever hot enough for me.

I would like to tell Mémé this. To tell her this and many other things, but I fall back asleep and the Smurfs come back to chase me. And I'm running, I'm always running.

Chapter 4:

Draw Me a Sheep

Every finger in the room is pointing at me / I wanna spit in their faces / Then I get afraid of what that could bring / I got a bowling ball in my stomach / I got a desert in my mouth / Figures that my courage would choose to sell out now.

— Tori Amos, "Crucify"

I'm eight years old and I'm in second grade. In second grade, on the second floor of the school that is two streets from my house. It seems complicated but it's not. To get to my school, you have to go past the tavern where the men are drunk as skunks. They give me dimes at eight in the morning, in front of the big church, Sainte-Marie, which is a million times bigger than me. It's not complicated to get to my school. No. The complicated part is that I can't go there by myself. My grandmother says because I'm too little, the drunks at the tavern will drag me into the bathrooms to make me touch their pee-pees, and after that you'll never see me again. She says crap like that all the time, the old fuck!

It's pouring rain outside. But in the classroom, up on the second floor, everything is sunny. Everything is sunny because of the children's drawings.

BORDERLINE | 49

Their drawings are super ugly. Three-fingered moms; noseless dads; pets that look like toasters; purple trees; clouds with eyes and suitcases; windowless, doorless, chimneyless houses; cars as big as ocean liners; and grins! So many smiles...families with vacuum-cleaner-salesman smiles. The drawings are The American Way of Life, Québécois style. On my sheet of paper it's The Russian Way of Life, The Concentration Camp Way of Life, Dorion Street-style.

My drawing has only two blue eyes, in the very middle of the page. Two sad eyes poking out of the white paper. Blue and white. That's all I did, and I've completely traumatized the class. Doesn't take much. Bunch of wimps! Bunch of grass-grazing sheep! No kid wanted to sit beside or beneath my drawing. "The eyes are watching me!" they complained. "The eyes are following me!" they bawled. Scaredy-cats! So my teacher put my drawing behind the class, in the coatroom. Where she's sure no one will see it.

Normally, the other children all want to sit near my drawings, so they can copy them. They want to copy them because I'm always the one who wins all the contests with my hyperrealistic portraits of boring reality. Yeah! I'm really amazing at drawing...because I started forever ago! I think I started to draw two days after I was born, because I was so bored, because I knew if I wanted to survive it was better to invent a world. After my Cubist period, where I drew stupid cubes you had to stick into stupid moulds, I became an Impressionist. At three years old, I was an Impressionist who left an impression on everyone with my drawings. Hours and hours of drawing my little Fisher-Price figurines, my naked Barbies, the cigarette butts in my mother's overflowing ashtray, kitchen knives, my grandmother yelling at me, my mother crying. I drew everything. I even drew myself Christmas presents in case my mother wasn't allowed out of solitary confinement to buy me any toys. So I have a knack for drawing. So when my teacher says: *Draw me a boat*, I get to work. And there, my drawing's done, and it's the *Love Boat*, with all the characters. The captain, bald as an egg; Washington, the bartender, whose two front teeth have such a big gap you could fit a doorknob between them. The doctor, who always reacts to everything way after everyone else; and the good-for-nothing skinny redhead who shows her big teeth. The teacher says, *Draw me a sheep*. In no time flat I've drawn my sheep. Not a sewing machine! Not a column, a penis, or a Vinier! But a real sheep that goes *bahhh bahhh* if you've got enough imagination. The teacher says, *Draw me a family*. I reproduce the perfect family: dad, mom, dog, cat, house, pool, the whole kit, but a hundred times better than everyone else's. My daddies don't have three fingers, but five on each hand; my pets don't look like toasters, they look like real animals; and my houses have a door, four windows, and even a mailbox. I'm amazing at representing reality. But this time I went too far into the representation of reality. Today, I became a Surrealist. I broke through the borders of second-grade artistic audacity and scared the shit out of them. But I only drew what the teacher asked for: *Draw the first thing you can think of.* So that's what I did. Two sad, blue eyes. It was either that or a big doughnut dipped in chocolate, because I'm really hungry. I didn't eat this morning.

When I showed my drawing to the teacher, she felt uncomfortable. She looked around her, at nothing, and didn't know what to say to me. She rubbed her nose, her eyebrows, her bra, Alouette! It was like she was itchy all over. As if she had sprouted chicken pox. I stood there, waiting to hear what she usually says: *Oh! Sissi! Your drawing is perfect! Your drawing is so nice! Your drawing is my favourite drawing in the whole world!* I waited for her to say a few words that would grow my invisible little Princess Sissi crown, but she said nothing. Minutes passed, and she kept scratching herself all over. I waited, as usual, in front of her desk, with my big, ugly smile. I have a really ugly smile. I have a little clown mouth and big teeth. My teeth grew in too big. It's so ridiculous. It looks like I want to bite life with my teeth when, honestly, I'd rather puke life. I'm eight years old and life is already giving me indigestion. But anyway.

After much rumination, the teacher finally said: *Yeah... Sissi... your drawing... uh... it's very original... um...* For the first time since I've shown her my drawings, she just said

52 | BORDERLINE

"original" and not "amazing," "marvellous," "magical," or "extraordinary." Original! So I've clearly traumatized the teacher with my drawing. I've traumatized her, except she has to hang it anyway, the old hag. She has to hang it like the others' so I don't feel sidelined, the way I do way too often. So sighing, she hung it on the wall with loud and smelly sighs stinking like a metro air duct with bad breath. She put it up while making an effort not to look at the two eyes. The teacher, traumatized. I don't care! Honestly, the entire school was traumatized by my two sad, blue eyes. Even the principal, who always hugs me in her arms when she sees my pretty drawings, was traumatized. She didn't know what to say when she saw it. No elementary school principal words came out of her mouth. She froze, her lips half-open, her arms falling at her side and her eyebrows down to her chin, not saying a word. Not a word. Silence. Silence, as usual. Silence, like at my house. Silence, like my mother's, staring at me with her blue eyes. Hours of staring at me beneath the pee yellow of the kitchen light without blinking. Ever. Forever.

My eyes are riveted to my desk, they won't detach themselves from the scratched, plastic, fake-wood surface with three cigarette burns. I can't hear what the teacher is saying. I don't understand what she writes on the black-board, either: numbers, letters, lines, geometric shapes, and bits of string. I can't tell if this is math or macramé. I can't... I'm unable to concentrate. I'm afraid. I'm having

BORDERLINE | 53

a hard time breathing. I'm having such a hard time breathing I think I'm going to have an asthma attack. A full-on asthma attack, with groaning, choking, rolled-back eyes, and all the rest of it! I think it's going to be a serious asthma attack because I forgot my Ventolin puffer. I left it someplace at home, on the dresser, I think, unless it's under my bed. I keep forgetting it even though *my grandmother's always saying: Sissi, don't forget your Ventolin, otherwise you might have an asthma attack, and that will worry your mother, and when your mother worries, she goes crazy, and then we have to lock her up. You don't want to make your mother crazy, eh?*

As much as she reminds me, I still forget it all the time. The Ventolin could be anywhere. It's not that I want to make my mother crazy and have her locked up in the psychiatric ward for eight months. It's not that at all. It's just that, despite being only eight years old, I must be suicidal. I must be suicidal like my mother will be in three years' time. Being suicidal must be in my genes. In my genes full of sick heredity. Even inside me, there isn't any space to breathe. I'm stuck in my stomach. My asthmatic lungs, since my last fever, always close up too much air. I will choke right in front of this gang of shits. Asthma is my new weapon, but I can't use it against anyone else. I'd like to give everyone a taste of it. But since there's only me to taste it, I might as well take advantage of it, and win the choke. Anyway, who would it bother if I died? I'm all alone in the world. All alone. I can already see my epitaph from here: *Here lies Sissi, the loneliest lonely person in the world. Go in peace, little mouse without a tail. The End.* I'm hungry. Hungry. I have full lungs but an empty stomach. I didn't eat this morning, because when I left home things weren't going well. They were not going well at all.

My mother and my grandmother were crying. It was grey outside. The weather was grey. The clouds even filled the house. The tap leaked. One drop per second. Drip! Drip! Drip! And again: Drip! Drip! Drip! A regular Chinese torture. My mother's and my grandmother's cries filled the whole house. Their cries and the dripping tap. Water everywhere. A big sad bath. I wanted to cry, too, but not for the same reasons as them. I don't know why they were crying. They cry all the time. My mother and my grandmother tell each other stories and cry. Sometimes they don't tell each other stories but they still cry. You'd think they were crying just to kill time. Fuck! I wanted to cry, too, but I had a reason. A good reason. I knew that if my mother didn't stop crying, she wouldn't be able to get me to school on time and I'd be late. I wanted to cry because I wanted to go to school. I must be the only kid east of Papineau Street who cries to go to school, who cries to sit at a desk, in front of a fake wooden table covered in scratches and cigarette burns. The only kid who cries to have a teacher, pencils, and loose-leaf paper and homework so she can busy herself, fuck! I wanted to cry

BORDERLINE | 55

because I was afraid of getting to school late, of dropping my binder in front of everyone, and having people laugh at me. I hate when people make fun of me. My hands tremble, my legs go weak, and my skin becomes red and blotchy. I feel really bad, and the worse I feel, the redder I turn. I hate when that happens, I don't know where to look, I don't know what to do with myself. I know, because people often laugh at me. They laugh at me because I have an accent, because I I ar-ti-cu-late when I speak. They say I'm fancy. "Heyyy, Fancypants, helllooo, Fancy!" They laugh at me and at my diction classes, on Tuesdays and Thursdays, during lunch hour. My diction classes to keep me from saying *sthlip, sthlide, lathethes*. All the "s," "sh" sounds get mixed get mixed up in my head, like the family roles at home: my mother is my sister, my grandmother is my mother, and my stepfather's a fucking dog, my grandmother always says. They also laugh at me because I'm skinny and my hair is like spaghetti and you can see through it when the sun shines. They laugh at me because my eyes are too big, as big as a pitiful dog's eyes. A beaten dog. *Sad puppy! Sorry mutt!* They yell. Or they laugh at me because of my name: Sissi. "Hey, Pissy!" Or, even, "Suck this, Sissy!" That's the grade fives. They also laugh at my dysfunctional family name, the name left behind by my grandfather Labrèche, who died of lung cancer at Notre-Dame Hospital some sunny Sunday afternoon. They call me the Suck, the Staple,[16] the Brush.[17] But they don't get it. They're not laughing at the right thing. My name means "the hole."[18] It's the cleft, it's the slit in my little body, the fissure that will lead me astray when I get older. Anyway. They've got plenty of time to laugh at me about that.

So I wanted to cry because I didn't want to be late and get laughed at. But also because I didn't want to miss my gym class with my bearded teacher. My teacher who is so nice to me. My teacher who ties my shoelaces so my sneakers don't break my face when we run in circles in the big room, run in circles like the nuts at the psych ward, that's what my grandmother told me. They make the crazies run in circles at the psychiatric institution during weekdays to keep them busy, so they don't try to kill each other or kill their families when they go home. I didn't want to be late because I wanted to run in circles and for my bearded teacher to tie my shoelaces. I wanted him to come close to me and look at me with his kind, brown eyes framed by his big, kind eyebrows. I wanted him to lean over me so that his shoulder would brush against my little body. To be less alone, for a few seconds.

There I was, in the middle of the kitchen, waiting for my mother to take me to school, but she wouldn't stop crying. She cried and cried. And when she eased up a little, my grandmother would start up again. So my mother would be back at it. You would have thought my mother and grandmother held all the world's sadness, that morning. You

BORDERLINE | 57

would have said they were hidden in a cave, in a country caught in war, during a bombing, that morning. And I stood there, in front of them, with my coat on, squirming for them to notice my hurry, but nothing worked. One minute my mother, crying like a real loser, got up from her chair and took me by the hand, the next she took her mother by the hand and laid us down in the bed. I lay between my mother and my grandmother, in the heart of tragedy. The best place for the show, with Dolby surround sound. And then the two of them went back to crying. And the tears ran, and I was soaked, and that made me want to go to school all the more. It wasn't my place to be there, in the middle of this bubble of tears, this bubble of madness. This damn suffocating bubble. This damn murdering bubble, filled with hyper-toxic liquid. This fucking toxic bubble of a nuclear family on the point of a nuclear explosion. I exploded and burst the bubble. I exploded and cried and cried, and after having cried, I yelled. I scratched my grandmother and my mother. I wanted to rip out their eyes so that they would stop crying, so that they would stop looking at me with their worried eyes. Their worried eyes that put fear in my belly all the time.

"Môman! Môman! Please! Take me to school! Come on, I'm going to be late, Môman! I beg you! I beg you!"

On my knees, two hands clasped.

"Môman! Come on! Hurry up!"

After seconds that stretched as long as the lines at

Steinberg's[19] during dinnertime, my mother wiped her eyes, dried her crazy tears, and extricated herself from the bed. She put on her wrinkled beige raincoat and brought me to school. I walked super fast the whole way. Sometimes I even ran. But my mother held my hand, her hand as soft as a cake that didn't rise, her hand as limp as badly baked cake.

"Hurry up, Môman! Hurry! I'm going to be late."

But she couldn't hurry any faster. Her steps were always so slow. You would have thought she was doing it on purpose. Going by Sainte-Marie Church, which is a million times bigger than me, and the tavern full of old drunks that was never as long and painful. All along, I was swearing, "Jesus-mother-fucking-Christ-fucking-goddamn-fucking-shit!"

And I pulled on my mother's hand, her hand limp as Pillsbury dough, and I swore again. "Jesus-mother-fucking-Christ-fucking-goddamn-fucking-shit!" An infinity later, I finally got to school. But by the time I got to my class on the second floor, it was too late. The students and the teacher were gone. No one was in the classroom. No one. Just the chairs, the desks, the blackboards, and the ugly drawings that seemed to make fun of me. The entire universe collapsed beneath me. My insides crumbled to the ground. I heard the giant sound of an empty stomach falling to the floor. I felt my heart slide down my thighs, followed by my other organs: my pancreas, my intestines, my liver, my kidneys. My mother looked at me and didn't say anything. She was blank. Erased.

"Say something, Môman! Say something! Help me. Môman! Say something! This is your fault! Everything that's happening is your fault!"

She still didn't say anything. So I kicked and punched my mother. I was so angry I wanted to stab her. If had had Luke Skywalker's lightsabre, a sabre as bright as a TV in the dark and as loud as a freezer, I would have chopped my mother in half, sliced her in two, and I would have thrown her evil-masked face into the fire. But I didn't have a sabre, just my fists, so I hit and hit and hit her with all my might. I didn't hit anything. My mother was totally erased. Fuck! My mother had become a hologram. Worse, my mother was a holocaust.

"I hate you, Môman! I hate you, Môman! If you only knew how much I hate you! My belly button hurts, I hate you so much! My birth hurts, I hate you so much! I should have hanged myself with my umbilical cord as soon as I came out of your crazy stomach! That's what I should have done!"

Just as I was saying these horrible things to my mother, my bearded teacher walked around the corner. He came up to me.

"What's the matter? What is it, my little Sissi? I was wondering where you'd gone. I was sure you wouldn't miss your gym class..."

He leaned towards me, still talking to me.

"You like gym, don't you? You're good at gym, aren't you?"

I knew he was trying to keep me busy, he was trying to get me to think of something else, so I would calm down. I bent my head. I didn't want to look him in the eyes. I didn't want him to see my eyes when they were angry, see my eyes throw fire. So I looked at my shoes. My pretty Pepsi shoes that made me a few centimetres taller, that brought me a few centimetres closer to the adult world. Fuck! I was tiny in stature, but I didn't even need to grow, I was already a thousand years old.

"Come with me, Sissi. Come on."

He held my hand very gently and we walked together. I turned my head and looked over my shoulder at my mother. She stayed there, unmoving. She looked at the ground, her two hands in the pockets of her wrinkled beige raincoat, her long black hair covering her face, her shoulders crumbling over her skinny body. I watched my mother until the hallway turned and I couldn't see her anymore. I wanted this to be a turning point of my life. I wanted it to last forever.

My bearded teacher brought me into the gymnasium. The other students were already there, running in circles like the psych ward nuts. He helped me get undressed and into my gym clothes. He took me by the hand and said, "Come on, Sissi! We're going to run together."

BORDERLINE | 61

So me and the nice teacher ran together for a long, long time. He didn't let go of my hand for one second, not even when the class was over, he still held my hand and came to help me change my clothes. When the teacher came to get us, her second graders, he kept me a few seconds longer in the gym. Once my teacher and the other students started to leave, he looked me in the eye for a long time, leaned towards me and held me in his strong arms, tight, tight. He said, "I know it's hard for you, Sissi. I know." My empty stomach climbed up the length of my body and dropped back into place; so did my heart, my pancreas, my intestines, my liver, and my kidneys. Things resumed a semblance of normality. A semblance of normality only because right now, things are not okay. At my plastic desk, my scratched-and-with-three-burn-marks desk, I'm choking. My lungs are holding too much air. It's like I'm buried in a pipe and I can scratch with my nails as much as I want, but the metal is too tough. I start to breathe harder and harder, louder and louder. I have to do something. I'll have to ask the class to get me a coffin or take me to the nurse.

Just as I'm about to lift my head to tell the teacher that I have to go to the nurse because I'm having an asthma attack, I spot her. In the doorway. Her. Her again. She's there. In the window. Her undone face pressed against the glass. Her eyes are frightened. The movements of her head are too quick to be normal. Strands of her black hair slice her face into strips. It looks like she's in prison, like she's trapped in the elementary school hallway. All of a sudden, I understand. It's all clear. The crying this morning. The sleepless nights. The meals she's stopped eating. And last night as we were watching TV, the two of us, she said, "Talk to Bernard Derome.[20] Tell him I love you. Go on, tell Bernard Derome that I love you." Bernard Derome was the news anchor. That's what was playing. That was it. Her madness started to take over her brain. Her madness exploded there, right there, in real time, in her little window of the second-grade classroom door.

All the other students turn and look at me: *Sissi, your mother is at the door! Sissi, your mother is here.* Yeah, my mother is there. Way too there. She's always there to spoil my life, to ruin my existence, to make my life a ball and chain to drag around, like when she starts to scream: Give me back my daughter! *Give me back my daughter! Bunch of Chinamen! Judas stealers! Return the flesh of my flesh! God sees all and will punish you!* She screams these vile phrases and bangs the glass. She hits it with all her might. Her long, white hands slap against the glass door. Every hit makes a dry bang! Bang! Bang! Every knock hits me and pierces me like a big, rusty nail hit from a big, rusty hammer. And the other students: *Sissi, what's the matter with your mother? Sissi, what's with her?* I'd like to scream: *Shut up, you bunch of shits! You bunch of little fucks who can't draw! So what, my mother's not like yours! So what, my*

mother's crazy! What the fuck do you care? Go fuck yourselves!
Get buggered by some bugs!

But I can't speak. I can't speak anymore. My lungs are in my mouth and my blood, throbbing in my veins, ever since the morning, projects me to the back of the classroom. In fact, I project myself to the back of the classroom. My blood, my hair, my big, ugly teeth in my little clown mouth, my feet, my hands. My entire little eight-year-old girl-carcass is now spread out on the back wall, I can't do anything about it, I can't even have an asthma attack. Everything stops. Time is suspended. In a final gesture, I lift my arms into a cross.

My mother just crucified me. She just crucified me in the coatroom. Where no one can see me.

Chapter 5:

Borderline

A pervasive pattern of instability of interpersonal relationships, self-image, and affects, and marked impulsivity beginning by early adulthood and present in a variety of contexts.
— DSM-IV, "Borderline Personality Disorder"

Anyway, I told myself I'd quit everything. I'd be a good little girl. Calm. Not one bit nervous. I'd be serious in my studies, in my loves. I'd tiptoe carefully in my little shoes. I told myself I'd quit drinking, at least cut down to two-three—four-five-six brandy glasses per day. No more. I'd put water in my wine and beer. I'd get in shape, get healthy, get pretty. Exercise at least three times a week at the YMCA, all the while taking care to wipe every machine after each use, as the rule on the wall indicates. And I told myself I'd take out my garbage, clean out my closet, my shed, my memories. Air out my fucking universe. That I'd be more pleasant with others. No paranoia. Study each situation coldly and objectively so as not to want to punch those who say bad things about people who are on welfare. I wouldn't cry in public anymore, in parks, on metros, or in shopping malls, because it bothers those who say bad things about people on welfare. I'd be considerate of my

BORDERLINE | 65

neighbour and reduce, reuse, recycle. I'd watch what I eat: no more saturated fats because they saturate the stomach. I'd cut out the microwave dinners because they leave a nuclear aftertaste. Cut the crap out too: no more chocolate, chips, no Vachon cakes while watching TV because they make your ass balloon. I'd be more productive: do more in less time. To be faster, I'd learn to drive a car, a motorcycle, a bus, a plane, and an ocean liner. I'd keep a fictitious diary to type up my thoughts in order to contain them, mark them. Check myself. That I'd be friends with the whole world, love dogs, cats, immigrants, and extraterrestrials, the whole parade, even double amputees. I'd call my old friends from primary school that I'd hurt in the schoolyard and I'd apologize, and they wouldn't remember what I was talking about and then I'd hit them to remind them. I told myself I'd watch what I say, speak more politically correctly: not say "black guy with a tape deck," but "a member of an audiovisual minority." I told myself I'd stop everything: the Sun from warming, the Moon from shining, the clouds from moving, the mountains and the winters from killing, the oceans from being wet. I'd stop everything: the masculine noun and the adverb, adjective, and pronoun. I was going to stop everything to be. Better. Good. Pretty. Perfect. A bitch. In a laboratory. Breathing carbon monoxide.

I did tell myself this. A year ago ... for real. I swear. But then there was this guy, with his curly hair, sitting on the foot of my bed, who put his fingers in my mouth. Then another guy, with Indian blood, who beat a drum on my stomach. Then the other guy with his guitar, he was unbelievably skinny, and he shook his hair in my eyes. Then the guy who wanted to marry me, give me children, buy me a bungalow, an in-ground pool, two lawn mowers, four Dobermans, and at least a hundred vibrators to make up for what he lacked... And the two guys at the same time, who couldn't stop touching me in the golden glow of the streetlamp.

And there was this girl.

This girl as blonde as me who kissed the palm of my right hand one night when we were drunk as two... drunk girls. This girl I met in a poetry class and who I'm still waiting for. All the time. Right now. I'm waiting.

I'm sitting on the counter of my pseudo-kitchen in the pseudo-loft I just rented with the pseudo-boyfriend I just met and I'm waiting. And to make sure I don't do anything other than wait for this girl who's affected me so deeply, my two hands are flat on my thighs. I'm waiting. Waiting is a constructive activity. Constructive... because while I'm waiting, I'm building boats in my mind. Beautiful boats and beautiful castles in the sky. I'm good at that. I'm fucking great at it! My grandmother always told me: *You're fucking great at telling stories. You're fucking great at telling stories that make your mother crazy...*

Stories that make my mother crazy... I'm good at those.

I've got years of practice. I construct everything carefully, my boats and my castles, with nails and hammers. I put a lot of drool and elbow grease into it. But, just like in the story of the three little pigs, each time there's a big gust of wind, a breath of stinking air, it wrecks everything and I'm the one in a thousand pieces on the ground. Maybe because I'm a little pig, too? That's what my grandmother often said: *You're just a little meanie and a little pig!*

A little pig and a little meanie who made her Barbies take their clothes off at Cindy's house. My Cindy house was just a big brothel. A huge brothel in the clouds of my bedroom, like my boats and my castles in the sky.

I can't say that my boats and my castles are better than real life because everything looks the same. When I close my eyes it's dark. When I open my eyes it's dark. Everything is black. Like right now. Only the glow of a big streetlight cuts through the curtains and lights the pseudo-loft I rented to fuck in. Everything is black. Like I was caught in one of the black holes in space. Like if that black hole had gravitated around me in those years and that it had, in one moment of inattention, aspirated. So everything is black. Always black. Except for Saffie's blonde hair. I'm waiting for her.

I don't know what it would be like to spend the night with Saffie. I don't know. So I'm nervous and excited, but that doesn't mean anything—I'm always nervous and excited. Being nervous and excited is part of my personality.

It's part of my sick personality; sick because I've started therapy, and the therapist, all slouched in his armchair, told me I have a sick personality. A personality with the flu. No, worse, I have personality cancer: a tumour inside me that's been feeding on my cells since I was a little girl. And, as it was not taken care of early enough, I'm stuck with it forever, until the end of time, until death. I'm borderline. I've got a problem with limits. I can't tell the difference between inside and out. Because my skin is on backwards. Because my nerves are tightly wound. I think everyone can see inside me. I'm transparent. I'm so transparent I have to scream so people can see me. I have to make a racket for people to take care of me. That's why I don't know when to stop. That's why I speed through life at two hundred thousand miles an hour. That's why everyone wants to give me a ticket when I'm running through the living room. I break everything. Demolish everything. Limits are too vague. Fuzzy. My reality distends itself. I err into a sphere that isn't full of air but of sex and beer. Nothing is definite in my life. Who I am, what I'll do, what I'm worth, who I'm into: men, women, little birds. I proceed by elimination. So for tonight I'll say I'm into women and little birds. Because Saffie's on her way over. There. I can hear her coming up the pink staircase in the building where I live. Her step is lively. It's going to be a nice night.

I open the door. I'm as excited as a young virgin. Saffie comes in. She's as excited as a flea on a poodle. We can't stop laughing. We can't stop interrupting each other. We can't stop moving around for no reason. We sit down.

"Oh, look at the painting I bought..."

We stand up.

We sit down.

"Oh! Look at this photo my friend took..."

We stand back up.

We sit back down.

"Oh! What do you want to listen to?"

"I don't know? What do you have?"

"I've got...and..."

We stand back up.

We sit back down.

It goes on like that until our third glass of wine. Suddenly. Bang! The alcohol hits. We stay sitting down.

The pasta's ready. We eat a little. Fettuccine Alfredo. I watch her suck up the long noodles that stretch straight from her plate to her stomach. I think Saffie's pretty, even with her mouth full. I'm not hungry. I barely eat. She tells me about her friends in Quebec City, her family in Quebec City, her dog in Quebec City. I barely listen to her. It's too hard to concentrate. I can't stop thinking about her. It's strange. I can't stop thinking about what she told me: *It's a girl crush—we've got girls' love at first sight.* Girl crush. I don't know what she means by that. Friends? Lovers? I don't know, but what I do know is she moves me, shakes me. She throws me off my chair, even if I'm still sitting

70 | BORDERLINE

very straight while holding my fork on which my fettuccine dangles.

After supper we go out. We go to a bar. We don't have much choice. My pseudo-boyfriend just got back and started to blather about his pseudo-crap. He doesn't like Saffie. You can tell. He doesn't like her because he doesn't like my choices. So me and Saffie get out. We go down my pink staircase. We open the door to my building; we're in the gay village.

We walk a little. It's winter. It's cold as a witch's tit but I don't feel anything even though my coat is wide open. Anyway, tonight I could get my rib cage smashed in and I wouldn't feel anything.

We find a cute bar; it's tiny. We sit down, across from each other, and we drink. We talk, we laugh, and we drink. We talk, we laugh, and we drink. But after a while I can't stand looking at her too-pink lips pressed against her red wine glass.

"Saffie. I want to go to a hotel with you. I want to sleep beside you, I want us to eat eggs for breakfast tomorrow morning...eggs and toast..."

Saffie smiles at me.

"Me too."

The hotel we find is pathetic. It looks like a gas station. When the guy at the front desk sees us strut up in our heels, two blondes together, he gets excited. He's excited, he stutters, he laughs for no reason. He won't stop showing us his big horse teeth. I think he looks ridiculous, all the more so when he keeps dropping everything on the counter. He's completely destroying the hotel, he's so excited about us being there. After a thousand and one arabesques, he finally holds out the keys to the room, gives us a big smile, a big solicitous smile. Just imagine his teeth!

With the lights on, the room is so crappy you could cry. The lights off, the room is as wonderful as *The Wonderful World of Disney*. We take turns in the shower, lying down on the bed. We have a little wine. I'd already thought of that. We drink from the same glass. Then from the same bottle. Then from each other's mouths. I take a sip of wine and pour it into her mouth. She takes a sip of wine and pours it into my mouth. The gulps get bigger and bigger and our mouths open wider and wider. Tongues push the wine into our throats. I lift the white sheet. Her body is like mine. I can't get over it. Same waist, same breasts, same hair, same laughing eyes. Am I touching myself? Am I in a full-on narcissistic crisis? Am I lying on a mirror? Will the mirror break? Will I drown? It's absurd, but all of a sudden, I'm afraid. My throat tightens. Saffie puts her hand on my breast and opens her mouth very wide, wider still. She uses my oesophagus like a straw. She uses my oesophagus to drink from my stomach. She drinks my fear. Her breasts swell when they're touched; mine do too. It's funny, like four balloons touching.

I'm on all fours over her and I kiss her stomach. She's

soft. The city glow lights the room a little. I can see her blonde duvet. She moves as if she was being rocked. Her legs open; mine too. We're both completely spread wide. I lower my head. My tongue darts into her belly button, darts back out. Then my tongue draws little paths of drool from her belly button to her groin. Our legs open again, hers don't stop opening, I'd never have believed that legs could spread that far. It's like we want to put hole against hole. She moans. It's pretty, how she does it. I get back up. I see her eyes open. Her big cow eyes. I move up a bit, I kiss her breasts. Then she kisses mine. I'm so excited I'm going to explode. I'm going to erupt all over this pathetic room. I can't stand it anymore. I want her. I want her so much my stomach hurts. But when I stop myself and look at her, I'm afraid. Again, afraid. She looks too much like me. Something's not right. Is this girl my clone? Worse, am I her clone? Am I her subject and she's back to claim me and she needs me because she's sick and condemned? What if she's there to reclaim my liver, my spleen, my heart? What if, all my life, I've only existed to save hers? What if my function was to be a bag of organs? Her bag of organs? No! She won't have me! It's out of the question! I'll slash her face so much that no one will ever be able to recognize her. I'll shove my fist down her throat all the way to her stomach. I'll break her spinal column in two. I'll put wine bottle shards in her hole ... I'll ... Stop thinking, you fucking nutcase, I tell myself. It's just stress. It's just nerves. This always happens to me when I find myself in a new situation. Look at her. She doesn't want to hurt you. She just wants you to touch her. Look at her squirm. She just wants you to caress her.

Saffie blinks her eyes and smiles at me. I smile at her.

I move my hand on her hole and I push a finger in. Then two. Then three. Then nearly my whole hand. If I could I'd push my wrist in, my forearm, my entire arm, my shoulder, my torso, my neck, my head...I'd settle inside her. I make circles on her belly with my fingers. I've always liked that, circles on my belly with fingers. I tell myself she must like that too. She sounds like a dreaming puppy. I stop all movement and get up. With one arm I pull her towards me. She sits up, at the end of the bed, limp, ready in any moment to collapse, sinking on the bed. But I want her to stay straight, and I show her this with the strength of my hand.

I spread her legs and bring my mouth to her hole. It's the first time I've done this. It's soft. I've never gone this far with a girl before. Never. Her liquid runs in my mouth like sweet candy. Her liquid runs on my tongue and rolls on my palate while her smell takes over my brain. I'm very excited. Saffie is very excited. Sitting on the edge of the bed, she squirms like a cat stuck to a fence. I continue to move my tongue. Saffie seems to turn into herself. She almost flits through the room. On all fours, between her legs, I watch her. She caresses her breasts over my head. She caresses them hard, I see. She moans endlessly, without ever catching her breath. It dizzies me. My head is spinning. My stomach hurts. What's happening? I keep moving my tongue mechanically while I try to hide in my head. It's going too fast. Everything is stressing me out. My nerves are going to crack. It's because I saw another blonde girl in the room. But a smaller one. I saw a little blonde girl flit through the hotel room. Three girls in one hotel room, that's too much. It's too much for me. I'm going to get up and run away from here. I try to get out but Saffie grips my head between her hands and traps me. She cries out.

❊ ❊ ❊

Now it's calm. Now it's quiet. She's sleeping. I'm lost. That was making love to a woman. Just that. It wasn't enough. Something was missing. She was missing something. After she cried out, she tried to take care of me. She tried well enough, but she didn't have any energy left, her heart wasn't in it, and it annoyed me, I felt I was too much, out of place. There was too much noise in my head for me to concentrate. So I said we would sleep instead. She agreed. Now she's sleeping. She sleeps and snores like a little girl who snores. The curtains of the pathetic room are half-open. It's snowing. I can make out Place Dupuis between the fat snowflakes. It reminds me of university. How will it go on Tuesday? Me. Saffie. Sitting next to each other in poetry class? It makes me think of later, too. I'll go back to my pseudo-loft and my pseudo-boyfriend will be there. He won't yell at me because I cheated on him with a girl, because I broke his heart for a girl. No. He'll shut up and fuck me. Fuck me because he'll have spent the night thinking of his girlfriend, the girl he says he loves more than the whole world, going at it with another girl he could love more than the whole world. He'll fuck me with vim and vigour, and his movements will calm me. His dick and his back-and-forth movements will calm me. I'll be on familiar ground and nothing will happen to me. After the lovemaking, his lips will be bloody, he'll have bit them so hard. Mine will be swollen. Just swollen and calm. Calm because I know the rules with guys. With girls, it's different, it's complicated. With Saffie, the rules of the game are mixed up. Saffie wants experience; she wants to know what it's like to get it on with another girl. And that, I'll learn at my own cost, is only a matter of time. For the moment I am part of her experimentation. I feel, suddenly, that I am her little guinea pig, and it's just like in a laboratory, everything has its number, everything in its time and place, and those kinds of feelings are well guarded. While for me it's a mess in my feelings. I undo myself and remake myself as my stories unfold. I'm a circus girl on a silver wire, without a net, on the brink of falling. The limits are too blurry. Like I said, I'm borderline.

Chapter 6:

My Grandmother, the Blocks, and a Few Tests...

I tell him that when I was a child my mother's unhappiness took the place of dreams. That my dreams were of my mother, never of Christmas trees, always just her.

— Marguerite Duras, *The Lover*

I'm seven years old and I'm walking through the halls of Notre-Dame Hospital. My grandmother's holding my hand. Her hand grips mine tightly. Very tightly. If she didn't restrain herself, I think she'd rip my arm off, the old nut. She's hurting me and I'm complaining. "Mémé, it hurts!" But she can't hear anything. "Fuck, Mémé, you're giving me a booboo!" Even when I swear, she doesn't hear me. My words are muted by the constant flow of phrases escaping her mouth, like a kind of grumbling. Thunder rumbling over my head. My grandmother mumbles things I don't understand. But it's not important, she must just be talking crap.

"I had enough with one, but not two! No, they can't take her! I'll fight! I'll hide her."

"Hey, who are you going to hide, Mémé? Who?"

She doesn't answer. I don't care. We walk quickly. The hallways smell like sickness and my grandfather's death. Here in Notre-Dame Hospital is where my grandfather died. In Notre-Dame Hospital, one Sunday afternoon in May. It was sunny. I wanted to play outside but I wasn't allowed to. I had to stay in the waiting room in intensive care. Nurses took care of me. I remember. I played hide-and-seek with the nurses and my blue doll. My neighbour, the witch, gave me my blue doll one day, when I must have been crying for a doll. I loved my blue doll, who died with my grandfather, more than anything in the world, even more than my two crazy mothers. After my grandfather died, I left the hospital holding my mother and my grandmother's hands, and after that I never saw my blue doll again. Not once.

Every time I visit my mother, every Sunday when I walk through the hallways of Notre-Dame Hospital, I look carefully thinking I might find my doll. I know we threw her out because they were afraid I'd get germs. But I still hope she might be here. I know I'm just telling myself another story to add to the multitude of stories I tell myself. There's a bag full of stories in my head. A bag full of pretty stories where I'm a princess and I get all the gifts in the world, even the new Hawaiian Barbie I saw the other day at Peoples I'd give anything to have.

Today, there's no way I can sneak through the hallways to try to find my blue doll, my grandmother's walking too fast, the brute. She walks so fast I'm having a hard time keeping up with her. My steps are too small. So I take one step, then two, then run. And again, one step, then two, and then I run. I can't wait to get there because I'm seriously tired. And on top of that, my grandmother woke me up very early this morning. She woke me up to stare at me. Great hobby! We sat in the kitchen facing each other, me in front of her wrinkly old bag, and she gave me my Flintstone vitamins. She gave me two and I crunched them happily. They're so good I'd eat the whole bottle. Then I ate my Raisin Bran and the entire time my grandmother stared at me, stared hard, as if it was the first or the last time she was looking at me. It gave me goosebumps.

I'm used to going to Notre-Dame Hospital. Very used to it, especially on Sundays: that's the day when kids can visit. Today is not Sunday, and yet here we are at the hospital, walking through the hallways. Usually, when we visit my mother, my grandmother makes me wear the salmon-coloured raincoat I hate more than anything on Earth. My grandmother says it makes me look clean and it makes my mother happy to see me wear it. The raincoat cost her an arm and a leg and if I don't wear it it's because I'm mean and I just want to hurt her, I just want her to waste her money and money doesn't grow on trees and I'm always pushing it with the bread and butter, I'm always asking for too much, I'm never happy with anything, I'm lazy, I'm sloppy, I'm going astray, I'll never amount to anything in life, I'll be on welfare with a husband who beats me and four kids in my arms, and blah, blah, blah. Normally when I come to the hospital it's to show my mother I'm wearing the salmon-coloured raincoat I hate so much.

When I get there, my mother is lying in her bed at Notre-Dame Hospital. She sits up and smiles at me. My mother looks like a junkie. A junkie who just got her fix. Her smile is as glassy as her expression. Her smile is empty, blank as her white skin. My mother opens her arms for me to throw myself into. I walk slowly towards her extended arms. I never throw myself. My mother is so fragile I could break her, tear her apart. I feel like there's a poster of my mother in front of me. But not a good poster. Not one where she's smiling, where she takes forever to put on some makeup, where she sleeps until two in the afternoon, where she complains that her feet hurt because she doesn't do anything. No, the other one. The poster of the dark days with big grey clouds.

My mother's arms, beneath the hospital's fluorescent lights, are covered with blue veins. My mother's arms are cold. That's another reason I don't throw myself into them. My mother's cold. Cold and effaced. Erased. But it's not her fault. It's because she's missing little bridges in her brain. That's what a doctor told me. Apparently, there are lots of little bridges in our heads that move words from one place to another. A few times a year, my mother loses a couple of bridges. So she goes to Notre-Dame Hospital for a tune-up, to get some repairs done. I'd say it's because her brain has already given her some free games, that's why we have to lock her up.

We're still walking through Notre-Dame Hospital, me and my grandmother, who grips me firmly by the hand. We're walking through the hospital, but for once I don't recognize the hallways we're walking through. That's because it's the Mailloux Pavilion, the crazy wing. We must be on the wrong floor.

"Mémé, aren't we going to go see Môman?"

She doesn't answer me and continues to mumble. So what! Keep your secrets to yourself, you old bitch! Seems like just this morning she was talking to me about my mother. I think. After I ate the Flintstone vitamins and my Raisin Bran for regularity, it seems to me that she said we were going to go see my mother. Or maybe she said that we would see if I was like my mother or against my mother? I can't remember. Anyway, my grandmother talks crap all the time. I was so tired this morning. My head fell off the table every two minutes. And my grandmother sat beside me in the kitchen, her arms leaning on the white tabletop, staring at me. She was nervous, and I was so tired. My eyes were shutting by themselves. She was yelling: *Finish your food! That way they can't say I don't feed you. They'll see that you're healthy. Finish your food!*

It's the first time I've walked through the hospital without my salmon-coloured raincoat. I'm glad. I'm finally dressed the way I like: in my black jeans with the Elvis guitar stitched on the right pocket, and my black turtleneck. I want to see what I look like in the windows when I'm walking, but it's the same deal as the blue doll, we're walking too fast, fuck! So I don't have time to catch my reflection in the hospital windows. Oh well! Later I'll go to the bathroom and look at myself a long, long time.

"Mémé, can we go to the cafeteria later?"

She doesn't answer me, the old meanie. I might as well be talking to a fucking plate of shepherd's pie!

"Are we going to the cafeteria later, Mémé? Say yes!"

"Yes, later, yes."

She answered me? If I'd known, I would've started talking to myself ages ago. I'm used to talking to myself, anyway. I've got years of practice in me. I spend my days soliloquizing. Like when I play with my little Fisher-Price figurines. I build houses with Lego blocks to house the Fisher-Price figurines, and they talk and they talk! It's a change from the constant silence that surrounds me. It's always quiet under the big yellow unshaded light in the kitchen ceiling. At least eight months of the year, while my mother is interned, and even when she's not! It's silent. That's when I build little houses with my Lego blocks for the Fisher-Price figurines and I imagine that's where my family lives and we're talking, we're happy, we're smiling, my mother isn't sick, and there are Christmas parties with lit-up trees and nicely wrapped presents, and lots and lots of people. The other day, I wanted to build a house for myself with my Lego blocks. But it only came up to my ankles. I didn't have enough blocks. I wasn't able to build myself a house.

"We're almost there," my grandmother muttered. "Stand up straight. Don't be nervous. Don't show all those fucking bitches you're nervous."

Two women stood before my grandmother and me. One young and one not so young. The young one was dressed in brown and beige and she smiled at me a lot. The other was wearing a white coat and seemed worried. My grandmother said a few words to them in a brittle tone. The older woman looked even more worried. I don't know what my grandmother told them because it's like there are sparks in my head. That always happens to me when new people look at me. I didn't understand what my grandmother said, but I could see the tone she'd used mustn't have been funny. Sometimes my grandmother can be tough. I know something about that. She can make all my friends run away with two, three words. They all leave with their heads down. Only I can hold my own with my grandmother, but I feel bad after.

"But, ma'am, please understand. Come with me. We'll talk it over. It's for the child's welfare."

"No, you can't have her," said my grandmother, agitated.

The child, that's me, I know it, but I don't know what to do. The woman wants to talk about my welfare with

BORDERLINE | 83

my grandmother. What's my welfare? Do they want to give me a cheque like my mother gets? My mother always gets welfare and that makes her well. She smiles. She looks relieved. She looks happy. If that's what it is, if it's because I'm also going to get a welfare cheque, well, okay! That'll be a good thing. I can buy myself the Hawaiian Barbie I saw at Peoples and help my grandmother who always says we're going to run out of money and we won't have any food to eat.

My grandmother finally lets go of my hand. It's about time. My fingers are blue. The blood's not circulating. She holds my hand tightly when she's nervous. Very hard. She doesn't realize it. The smiling woman says to come with her. I look at my grandmother to see if I'm allowed but she's staring into space. So I follow the young woman. We walk through the hallways, she asks me questions. I know she's trying to keep me busy, so I don't feel scared. She asks me what I ate this morning, what my favourite game is. She tells me I have nice pants, a nice pair of Elvis pants. She asks me if I know who Elvis is. Do I know who he is! I spend entire days in front of the mirror singing and dancing like him. I pretend I'm him, a big rock star and everyone loves me, and my grandmother is so proud of me she gives me lots of compliments. And I get money, too, just for singing songs. I make lots of money and I build a house for my grandmother and me, so we can have Christmas parties. But I don't tell the smiling woman any of this. Oh no, I know you can't tell people anything, because that's what my grandmother says. *Don't say things to people or they'll use it against you. It's never good to tell the whole truth. People might think you're crazy and lock you up the way they locked your mother up.* So I shut it and I keep my big rock star stories to myself. Anyway, I know it's just another story I tell myself. I tell myself too many stories. Too many stories. My imagination is overflowing from all sides like the colours of my colouring book. I have a thousand lives in my head. A thousand lives to hide in. But I don't tell the woman who's smiling at me any of this. I only tell her that I know Elvis because my mother has all his records and that he's the King of Kings. That's enough.

The woman who smiles at me a lot tells me her name is Aline. She asks me my name. Sissi. She thinks my name is pretty, it's like the empress, it's a princess's name. Everyone says that. Aline takes me to a sunny little room. Everything is white: the walls, the ceiling, the floor, the tables, the chairs. And the sunshine beaming through the big windows makes the room dazzle. It hurts my eyes. One large mirror adds a bit of colour to the room. Aline asks me to wait a minute. She leaves, goes to another room, then comes back. Her arms are full of blocks of every colour, of paper, Prismacolor, paints. She tells me we're going to have fun together. From the tone she's using to speak to me, I feel like she's scared I'll start screaming that I want to see my grandmother, that I want

BORDERLINE | 85

to get out of here. But she's wrong. She doesn't need to worry. Aline seems nice. Plus, she has lots of crayons, papers, and blocks. What more could I ask for? My grandmother? No way, she's totally nuts today.

Aline and I set ourselves up at the dazzling little white table. She asks me to draw a ceiling for her. I draw her a ceiling. She asks me to put a light bulb in the ceiling. I add a light bulb to the ceiling. She asks me what, exactly, a light bulb is for. I tell her it's to hold up the ceiling. She looks at me, disconcerted. *Come on, Aline, seriously. It's to light things up.* She breathes. She looks relieved. Aline asks me to draw a house and a family for her. I give her the whole kit: the family, the house, the cat, the dog, the lawn mower. I'm having a bit of a hard time with the in-ground pool because I'm starting to run out of space. Aline looks at my finished drawing. She seems stunned. I showed her.

Aline asks me why the daddy is painted all in red when the other characters aren't. I tell her it's because the grandmother threw a brick at him and he took it right in the face. He's lying on the ground and he's knocked out. Aline's eyes get bigger. I can tell she's interested in my stories. She can't get enough of them. I start up. And I go on for a while.

An hour, two hours, three hours go by and I don't stop talking. Drawing and talking. Drawing, putting blocks in little spheres and talking. And Aline asks me more and more questions. But then I start to get annoyed. It seems

like it's been a long time since I've seen my grandmother.
I start to find it suspicious. Aline looks at me and says:

"Hey! Your drawing's so nice! Your lamb is cute!"

"It's not a lamb, it's a lady elephant's Tampax!"

"Whoa! What did you say, Sissi? You're very pale!"

"It's because I ate toilet paper when I was three, fuck!"

"I think you're tired... You'd like to see your grand-mother, wouldn't you?"

"Yes."

"We'll go see her, come with me. You did a great job."

She takes me by the hand, walks beside me down the hallways of the Mailloux Pavilion at Notre-Dame Hospital. Her hand is soft and warm. Her hand is like a caress in my hand. Her hand isn't like my grandmother's, full of arthritis and ready to crush my joints. No. Aline holds my hand very gently, without squeezing it, without squishing my fingers. We walk slowly. I have time to look into all the other rooms as we walk by them. There are many children here. Most of them look funny. Some pull their hair while mumbling strange words. Others scream like they're being chased by an army of Martians. And others have the same glassy eyes as my mother.

We walk by a little office. Suddenly, I see my grand-mother is standing in front of the woman from earlier, who is also standing behind her big desk. The room is very well lit. Daylight fills the space so brightly that I can only make out the silhouettes of both women. My grandmother says, in a very hard voice, "You'll never get her! I'm going to fight!"

I feel her words and I'm uncomfortable. I don't like it when my grandmother acts so savagely. I'm embarrassed for her. I don't like it when she attracts attention like that.

Aline tells me to sit on the bench, there, beside the office. She goes into the office where my grandmother is and closes the door behind her. Only the door doesn't close properly, and I can hear everything they're saying, when the kids stop crying.

"No, ma'am, calm yourself," says the woman. "You've been on edge for three hours. We have the results."

Aline speaks. "Little Sissi is a hyperactive child... agitated, of course, with all the drama that surrounds her, but she is very creative. And the stories she tells are sane ...and...mental illness, like her mother...your daughter ...hospitalized..."

Then I can't hear anything. There are doctors going by with screaming children. Little shits. I want to scream, too, but I hold back.

I hold back. I hold back.

I hold back so much that I bite the inside of my cheeks with all my might. I don't want them to keep me here like they keep my mother. And I drew nice pictures. I told nice stories. And I did what my grandmother told me to do, I didn't tell them all the stories because they might use them against me. Against us, me, my grandmother and

88 | BORDERLINE

my mother. Against. I don't want to be here anymore. I didn't do anything wrong.

I look at my hands. I put them over my eyes and push hard while leaning my head against my thighs.

I sing:

C'est une poulette grise / qui a pondu dans l'église / Elle a pondu un petit coco / pour Sissi qui va faire dodo / Dodiche Dodiche...[21]

Chapter 7:

Borderline (Continued)

Individuals with Borderline Personality Disorder make frantic efforts to avoid real or imagined abandonment. The perception of impending separation or rejection, or the loss of external structure, can lead to profound changes in self-image, affect, cognition, and behaviour.
— DSM-IV, "Borderline Personality Disorder"

A week's gone by and I haven't called her. I don't know if she's tried to call me. I ripped out the phone cord. The loft has been silent, almost uninhabited. I was alone all week. Lost in my loft. Alone. I spent most of my time sitting in the middle of the apartment looking out the massive windows. I have three massive windows that nearly fill a whole wall. When it rains, during the day, the light is beautiful on my skin. It looks like I'm shimmering. It looks like I'm warm. Like I got fucked and I got hot. It's been a week since I fucked anyone. Not Saffie. Not my pseudo-boyfriend. No one. It's been a week since I had a drink, too. But it's been long enough. I'll have to buy a new phone cord.

"Sissi! I haven't heard from you in such a long time! I tried to call you all week! What happened? You didn't come to class, either!"

"I just needed to rest."

"But what happened?"

"Do you want to get together?"

"Hang on, I'm coming over."

Saffie shows up at my house. She comes in without knocking. She comes in like it's a barn. She comes inside me like a barn. I don't greet her. I stay put, on my spot, right in the middle of my loft. Sitting on the ground in the middle of my tragic kingdom. All that's missing is a crown of crap for me to be worthy of my name.

"What's the matter, Sissi?"

Saffie looks at me with enormous eyes. I can see the white around her blue irises. She seems discouraged. She looks at me the same way my grandmother did this week. My grandmother and I fought. My grandmother called me a thief. She thinks I stole her money. Three hundred bucks. She must have chucked it in a cookie jar or hid it under her mattress, but she doesn't even bother to look. No, she's convinced I pulled a fast one on her. "You're always going into my room and rummaging around." I rummage! I rummage! Of course I rummage! She hides everything: Kleenex, candies, family photos, magazines, calendars, cigarettes, everything goes in there. From the moment my mother was alive, my grandmother hid her purse in her room. If ever my mother wanted her own money, she'd have to ask Mémé for it. "Maman, can I have some change, I'd like to go to the dépanneur?" My grandmother has absolute

92 | BORDERLINE

control over everything. It reassures her, it comforts the wrinkled old bag. It makes her feel indispensable. I only feel indispensable when I'm getting fucked.

I catch Saffie by the arm. I just want her to curl up into a little doll on the floor beside me. I want her to curl up into herself and rock, but Saffie doesn't understand and doesn't want to. She wants words, she wants to know why I didn't call her. Why I'm messing with her.

"Saffie...you scare me. You scare me because I feel like I've met my double and you're going to kill me and take my place. Some tribes think that if you see your double it's because you're going to die soon. I think I want to die, just not yet. I need to prepare, you know?"

No. She doesn't understand, and what I'm saying scares her.

"Saffie, I'm begging you, read between the lines. Listen to what I'm saying, there's an emptiness in my stomach and I fill the emptiness with everything I can find. But most of the time, what I find is trash. That's why I'm always scared. That's why I'm scared of you. You're part of the stories I tell myself. You feed the stories I tell myself. Do you want to know what they're like, the stories I tell myself? They're tragedies that go sour, and everything turns out like a horror movie. And in my stories, I'm always the one who ends up the most damaged."

She doesn't understand this, either. She keeps looking at me, disconcerted, the way my grandmother looked at me this week. "What! You didn't steal the money! I know you're always going into my room" My grandmother's eyes can be so mean. Even meaner when the weather is grey, when the clouds are heavy and low. "I know you stole it. I don't know why you want to hurt me so much. You want to kill me the way you killed your mother, is that it?" The public housing rooms are greenish grey. The weather is humid, sticky. My heart is heavy. "No! Mémé! I didn't steal anything." But she doesn't believe me. She's never believed me. She doesn't believe me that I didn't beat my mother when I was five years old, that my mother was trying to escape when I was five years old. She doesn't believe me. In fact, yeah, I did beat her, my mother, but I didn't do it on purpose. I swear! I didn't do it on purpose. She wanted to catch up to my grandmother, who had gone to buy milk at the dépanneur. She wanted to go find her because she was in sock feet, in the middle of winter. And my grandmother had told me: *Don't let her out. She might get hit by a car.* I was so scared, and my mother was so strong in her craziness. And I screamed: "No! Stop it, Môman! Stop it!" My grandmother didn't believe me, like she doesn't believe I didn't steal the three hundred bucks.

"Saffie, let's party, okay? I think I'd like that!"

I get up, put a CD in the CD player and turn the music way up. Smashing Pumpkins at full blast. Let the neighbours knock! It doesn't matter. It'll be something concrete. I jump everywhere. I dance. I get dizzy. I want to lose myself. I want to disappear into thin air. No longer be. Saffie jumps with me. She doesn't seem to know why, but she does it.

"Hey, Saffie, I want to do something special, something crazy."

She smiles. I feel like she likes this little girl's game. I pull out a bottle of wine I'd put in the pantry just in case . .. After a week of holding back it's going to hit me hard! Me and Saffie drink the wine, not in each other's mouths this time but from glasses. We won't use our oesophaguses as straws. Then I run a bath. And we drink red wine in the bath. And for the first time this whole week I feel good. Sitting in the bath, all the loft lights out. The streetlight glow lights the loft and gives a sheen to my little kingdom. Fuck, it's beautiful! I pray so much for moments like this to happen more often. Hubert Aquin[22] would have wanted to live perpetually in the moment of orgasm, that's when he felt best. For me, it's moments like these: in the bath, drinking wine.

In the bath, Saffie and I compare our breasts. We could be comparing bowling balls, but it's still fun. It's a funny game. Her breasts are really similar to mine, maybe just a bit bigger. It's sexy. I move my hands and touch a little. She lets herself be touched. The problem with her is that she always lets herself be touched. She doesn't seem to take much initiative. But anyway ...

After the bath, we rummage through my clothes trunk

and decide to put corsets on. We look at each other in the mirror. We look like whores. We're pretty great. We've got potential.

"Hey, Sissi, you know what we should do, someday? We should pick up a rich dude together. We could make some money, don't you think?"

"Or we could rob a bank. We'd make more money, and faster!"

"Why are you talking so stupid?"

"Have you ever fucked someone you didn't like?"

"No."

"Try it, you'll see, it's no fun..."

"Have you done it a lot?"

We lie on the bed and listen to music, another record: Nine Inch Nails. I sing the songs into her ear: "He put the gun into his face...Bang! So much blood for such a tiny little hole..." And I put it on again: "I hurt myself today. To see if I still feel." She likes it. She smiles. She laughs, too, a little laugh. She turns me on, this girl. I keep getting wet. If this keeps up, I'll make puddles everywhere on the ground. I'm going to flood, I'm going to pour.

Saffie looks at me with her big cow eyes. Her long eyelashes bridge the gap between us. She waits. I feel like I don't turn her on as much as she turns me on. I think she's just going with the flow. She wants to see how far I can go for her. I play this game, too, but with men. I always want to see how far they're willing to go for me. My grand-

96 | BORDERLINE

mother also wants to see how far people are willing to go for her. She tests our limits constantly. In fact, she tested my mother's limits so much that one day my mother took all her pills while I was watching *Les tannants*. Maybe my grandmother's still testing my limits? Maybe to see how far I'd go for her, by calling me a thief. I can't think about my grandmother or my heart will collapse.

Just as we're starting to make love, just as I'm starting to caress her, and she opens her legs into infinity, my pseudo-boyfriend walks in. He wasn't supposed to get back from his homeland today. He was supposed to stay at least another week. He comes in and catches me in the act, my hand between Saffie's legs, fingers wet from her liquid. He's drunk. He doesn't look happy. But he's a nice guy, and his great tragedy, his great sadness, is that he loves me. So he swallows his pain. Looks detached. He raises his eyebrows and looks at us condescendingly. Saffie gets dressed quickly and she's laughing, but I can hear the discomfort in her laugh. She puts on her clothes at a vertiginous speed. I also put on my clothes at a vertiginous speed. But I could also not put on my clothes. Who cares? My pseudo-boyfriend looks at us, wide-eyed. His eyes don't seem to be looking in the same direction. I think he looks ridiculous. In fact, we all look ridiculous in this big room trying to hide from each other. It's hard to hide in a loft.

There's a strange moment when Saffie's finished dressing. A pause in gestures, in words, in looks. A moment where I feel I am uninvited. Saffie's standing in front of my pseudo-boyfriend. They're looking at each other. It lasts thirty seconds. Maybe less, maybe more. I don't know. I only know that in that moment, there's something going on between the two of them. They're in front of each other; they're silent. It hurts. Their silence hurts me. I want to break the silence, but my lips feel glued together. Only my facial muscles are able to contract. And yet in my head I'm yelling, yelling loudly. But my cry remains silent. I know… they don't love each other. My pseudo-boyfriend loves me. And Saffie loves me. He doesn't love her, and she couldn't care less about him. But now, it looks like another story's being written. Another story with another princess.

He says, in his big voice, "The three of us could do it. Eh, Sissi? Queen of the bedroom?" He says it again, in his big voice, not looking at me, staring at Saffie: All three of us could do it? Me. You. And Saffie.

I don't say anything. She doesn't say anything either. Her silence makes it clear that she'd like that, she'd like us to have a threesome. She'd like me to put my tongue in her mouth while he rummages around her hole and slobbers all over her body. I understand this from her silence. And I also understand that she was and remains a seductress. She wants the whole world for herself. The whole world in her belly so she can feel a little better. I look at her. She disgusts me. He disgusts me. In fact, they disgust me in every pronoun. They disgust me in every possible pronoun. They disgust me so much that it's become physical and I want to spit everywhere I look. A threesome! No. I don't want to do that with them. No. It would be like putting my head on the block and teasing the executioner. I can't watch Olivier kiss this girl who looks like me and could too easily take my place. And I can't watch this girl who's touched me, touched me so deeply, touch Olivier. No. Even though I know that ordinarily I'd be the first one to dive into the bed naked, even though I know that opening my legs to one, two, three, four people, to the whole world at the same time, isn't a problem, right now I don't want to. There's too much energy between Olivier and Saffie for it to be safe. There's too much energy between them for me to stay in first place. And second place, no thank you. I already gave too much. Too many years coming second after my mother . . . Now, I don't want to anymore. I can't. I'd rather not exist.

My mouth opens very wide. My eyes crinkle. I can hardly see, through my eyelashes, the scene that unfolds. Saffie stays standing in front of the man who said he loved me the most in the whole world. I get up. I have to scream. I have to do something so I'm not rejected. To not feel that I'm left by myself. And the words of my grand-mother that come back to me now: *If you chase two rabbits at the same time, you'll lose both of them.* I'm losing Saffie. I'm losing Olivier, my pseudo-boyfriend. I'm losing my grandmother with her story about the stolen three hundred dollars. No. I don't want to.

I throw myself with all my might at my big mirror. The big mirror I use when I'm making love. The big mirror that has confirmed my presence while I'm getting fucked. I break the mirror into a thousand pieces. My image disappears, but I'm still not anyone else. Unfortunately, I'm still myself. Rejected. Rejected. Rejected. Rejected. Rejected. Rejected.

Saffie and Olivier hurry over to me. There's blood on the pieces of mirror still hanging in the brown frame. The blood spreads over the wooden floor and onto my arms. Saffie and Olivier try to hold me. I push them away. I hit them with my feet and hands. I want to let it rip that they disgust me, but my mouth is as always open/closed, it does what it wants. My mouth is stubborn. Olivier and Saffie hold me tightly. I can't kick or slap them anymore. They lay me down on the bed. They're both on me. While they're on me, I hear them speaking. I think I hear them say: *We'll wait till she's asleep and then we'll make love. We'll make love. We'll make love right beside her when she's sleeping* ... They're like two sticky serpents beside me. If I don't do something their red viper tongues will prick me and I'll get infected. Finished. My strength quintuples. I'm Goldorak.[23] I'm huge and made of metal: "Screw crusher punch!" I free myself, I manage to find the door. I fall down the pink staircase of the building where I live ... lived. Because I

100 | BORDERLINE

won't come back. I'll never set foot on that perverted floor again. I won't breathe between those walls of lamentations. I'm leaving. I leave this place that was never my home anyway.

I walk. It's raining rats.[24] Even though it's winter. It's been warm for a week. Eight degrees in January, that's something. The weather's all upside down. Like an old refrigerator. I'm as off-kilter as an old refrigerator, too. So was my mother, in her time. Cyclothymic. If it wasn't nice out, my mother wasn't nice to look at. If it was nice outside, she bought me all the Barbies in the world.

I'm completely soaked. I walk without thinking. Out of habit, my feet take me to my grandmother's house. My grandmother. My only living relative spends her time denying me. My grandmother who just accused me of robbing her. My grandmother who isn't always nice to me. I'm in front of her little house with the salmon-coloured borders, I sit on her porch cross-legged in front of her door and wait. I'm not ready to go in, not yet. I'm afraid she'll throw me out. I'm never ready for that. So I sit cross-legged in front of the salmon-coloured door and wait. It'll be a while.

The rain is torrential tonight. And it's starting to get cold. Winter has decided to return while I'm outside, sitting in the snow on the porch. The rain permeates my clothes. I'm soaked like a chunk of doughnut in dirty dishwater. I'm going to get sick. I'm trembling all over.

Suddenly, my grandmother opens the door. Without saying a word, she grips my arm and yanks. I go into her house. I'm shivering. I'm so cold. My grandmother helps me take off my soaked clothes. I'm in my black corset, soaking wet in front of her. My grandmother sees that I'm hurt. There's blood and little pieces of mirror stuck to my shoulder. She tells me to lie down. I start to feel better when I lie down on the sofa. I start to get my colour back. My grandmother washes my wound with a washcloth. Then she hands me a little glass of red wine.

"Here, this'll make you feel better."

She doesn't know that red wine doesn't make me feel better but breaks me. But I drink the wine anyway. I start to feel sick to my stomach again, and nauseating images from earlier come back to me. What can they be up to, those two at the loft? They must be cheering and fucking. They must think I'm crazy. Crazy like my crazy mother, and that I should take pills too, like my crazy mother, to be done with life. I shake it off. I don't want to think about it. I want to sleep.

The next morning, I wake up with a start. A familiar sound wakes me. My grandmother's doing the dishes. She's doing the dishes like when I was little, like a fucking maniac. It reassures me, I feel okay. But not well. I'm afraid she'll accuse me of robbing her again. I sit up on the sofa. As soon as she sees I'm awake she brings me coffee with a lot of sugar and a little bit of milk. Coffee the way I used to drink it before I got complicated and started taking my coffee black, to lose weight, to have some style, to make myself suffer.

Sitting on the sofa, I take tiny sips of my coffee. My grandmother sits beside me on her rocking chair and rocks. It's the only sound in the house. The sound of her chair and the sound of the rain that's still pouring outside.

"Are you hungry?"

I say I'm not, although my intestines are screaming like lunatics. I'm afraid she'll tell me that as well as stealing her money I'm taking her food.

"You know...I found the money...the three hundred dollars. I'd put it behind the curtains."

Then she rocks even harder. She's nervous. The weather is grey. The rain falls harder. It drips down all the windows in the house. Through the windows, the rain projects the drips along the walls and onto my grandmother. It looks like a film is being projected onto her. A film with fuzzy actors.

"You can't be angry with me...you know I'm old and you're my only family."

She doesn't say anything else. She stares off into the distance and rocks a little more calmly now. I don't say anything either. I sip my coffee. It's hot and sweet.

Chapter 8:

Games without Frontiers

*I sat on my bed for a long time. I sat and sat. Something
was wrong inside me, I felt it in my stomach and I didn't
know what to do. So I lay down on the floor. I stuck out
my pointer finger and pointed it at my head. And I
pushed down my thumb. And killed myself.*
— Howard Buten, *When I Was Five, I Killed Myself*

I'm five years old and lying in my grandmother's bed.
She's babysitting me. My mother went to a wrestling
match at the Guy-Robillard Centre or the Marcel-Robillard
Centre or the Jean-Marc-Robillard, I don't know which. I
never remember stuff like that. What I remember is
Môman, Mémé, my dog Ponpon, my cat Magamarou, my
blue doll, three-coloured ice cream, and toys from Peoples.
I also remember that I can't piss my grandma off too much
when my mother goes to wrestling matches at the Tom,
Dick, or Harry-Robillard Centre, or else I'll be the one
getting the hammerlock and the Indian burn.

My mother's gone to the wrestling match with my
father. My father who's not my father. She went with my
stepfather, actually, my stepfather who isn't my stepfather,
either, at least not officially. He will be in a year. They'll get
married and not have a lot of kids. Just me. They'll think

BORDERLINE | 105

I'm enough. I'm worth ten kids, that's what they'll say. I'll be there when they get married. Running all over the place, under the fluorescent lights, in the too-big room at the courthouse. Dressed like a little flower girl. I'll wear a yellow dress, even though I hate yellow. I'll put flowers in my hair, even though I hate flowers in my hair because I'm not peace and love like my mother when she takes her antidepressants. I'll carry flowers, pretty little red and yellow flowers I'll want to eat throughout the entire ceremony to make it go by faster. I'm supposed to hold the wedding rings, that's what the morons told me, except when it's time to hold the damned wedding rings they'll take them away from me. Like I said, morons. They'll take away the rings in case I lose them because of my nerves. Because I'm a ball of nerves, because I move all the time, I yell all the time, and I laugh too loudly—I'm always roaring. Ha! Ha! Ha! Too loud. Mouth wide open, I alert the entire planet to my presence. Hey! Everyone! I'm here! Take care of me! Take care of me or else I'll do something bad. Look, my mouth is so wide open I could swallow the entire Earth in one gulp. My gestures are so abrupt I could unhook all the stars and make them drop out of the sky. And my cries are so piercing, so sharp, I'd break all the crystal in the galaxy if I wasn't constantly told, "Shhh! Shhh! You're going to bother the neighbours." They tell me that at least ninety times a day. They tell me so often that I sometimes swallow my screams to stop them from starting up about it again.

106 | BORDERLINE

But I'm excitable even when I swallow my yells. High-strung. It's my trademark. And, unfortunately for them, they can't exchange me for two boxes from the competing brand. They're stuck with me. Too bad. I'm nervous. It's written on my forehead and on my skin. I'm as nervy as the little poodle they bought me last year. A cute little poodle that yapped when we said its name: *Ponpon. Woof! Woof!* A cute little yellow poodle that ran after me everywhere and yelled with me. Me and the dog egged each other on. Being with the dog was like running in a marathon when everyone's yelling: *Go! Go! Go!* So we could go for hours. Hours and hours of fun, batteries not included. But one day, the morons had had enough, and they got rid of the dog. And to make it go down smooth as honey, they told me the dog had run away to find his mother. Weird way to tell me they brought the dog to the SPCA to have him put down, where his mother was probably killed, too. Anyway, with or without the dog, I didn't stop being excited and exciting others. I didn't stop making noise with pots and pans, balls, bells. Talking at the same time as everyone and very loudly, so that everyone would shut up and listen to me. And running, running, running, to make holes in the floor, to lose my breath behind me. I like running, I like it and I'm super good at it because I'm really fast. I'm faster than a comet, that's what my mother says when she's just taken her antidepressants. "You run so fast, Sissi! You're faster than a comet," she says with her protruding eyes and

BORDERLINE | 107

foolish smile. When she says that it just encourages me, and I redouble my efforts. My grandmother doesn't say I run like a comet. No. She says, "If you don't stop running like that the downstairs neighbours are going to complain and they're going to throw us out. We won't have anywhere to live, and we'll be homeless. Is that what you want?"

So what. I don't care what my grandmother says. I just keep running. Sometimes I run, and I throw myself at the wall, I don't know why, I just do it. Maybe I do it to make myself dizzy. Because when I'm knocked out time goes by faster. At my house, time seems stuck, it gathers in the living room and forms a thick fog around each of our bodies. It's heavy. When I wake up, I already want to go back to sleep. I'm only five years old but I notice it, everything is in slow motion, I'm not dumb, I'm not stupid. I'm not on antidepressants. I have a ceiling in my head. So I can see clearly that it's not going by fast, and everyone's bored stiff. At my house, life isn't a long, quiet river, but an artificial lake filled with PCBs. A stagnant lake. I see them, my parents, my two moms. They look frozen in space. They're like shadow puppets, sombre, their arms and legs contracted, always in slow motion. I see them, they're staring off into the distance, but they never talk, they never ever talk to me. The image is still. My family's VCR is perpetually on pause. But when I'm bad, the whole world stirs out of its lethargy and rushes to take care of me. I put myself on fast-forward and activate the house. A real Arnold Schwarzenegger in a skirt. *Fuck you, asshole!* Armed with my imaginary bazooka, I fire at everything around me to put them in all kinds of bizarre positions, so they don't swallow me up. Because everything is so big here. I break a glass, my mother screams in a soul-shattering voice that I did it on purpose and starts to sob. I pull a curtain down and my grandmother screams that I did it on purpose, that I want to break everything to hurt them. It's true, I'd wreck everything if I could. I'd trample all over the goddamned cockroach-covered cardboard house. I'd crush my mother's trapped-tragedy bedroom. I'd break all the disgusting, decrepit furniture into a thousand pieces to keep me from running off into infinity. But I can't, so I basically just run on the spot.

When I run and throw myself against the walls, it upsets my mother a lot. But she loves me, so she lets me do it. My mother loves me the most in the whole world. I know it and I take advantage of it. I want a doll, I get it. I want a Big Mac, I get it. I want to watch TV till I puke, I watch TV till I puke. I often take advantage of my mother—maybe even too often. My mother's afraid of me. I mean, she's afraid of everything. She's a victim. If she were an animal, she'd be a lamb getting eaten by a lion. If she were Russian, she'd live two steps from the nuclear power plant in Chernobyl. In a horror movie, she'd be the first to get her head chopped off and her arms and legs cut off and her intestines would be yanked out by the huge, sticky green monster. My mother's like that, she's got as much personality as a washcloth. But I'm not a victim. I'm not the worm you put on the end of a line to hook a big fish, so I really scare my mother. She's afraid of my screams and my cries. When I scream and cry, she's scared people will say she's not a good mother, or that she beats me. She's scared the neighbours will send social services and social services will take me away in a truck full of mistreated children. She's afraid of being taken to court, then to prison, to a cell full of women who like women and that she'll be forced to become their sex slave. That's what my mother's afraid of, that's why she lets me do anything I want. And with two antidepressants under her belt it helps her to forget, it helps her not be afraid, it helps her smile at life. My mother smiles.

But as much as my mother's afraid of me, she's even more afraid of her mother, my grandmother. My grandmother scares her because she asks everything of her. My grandmother asks all of life from her. But as far as marriage is concerned, my grandmother's out of luck. She doesn't want her daughter to get married. But for once, my mother won't listen to her. My mother will want me to have a father. She thinks it would be healthy for a little girl like me to have a real family. It would be good for my nerves. I might be calmer and more balanced. It's good, she tells herself, for a nervous little girl to have a strong family.

Strong! Strong! As together as the religious families on the religious calendars hung on the walls against which I throw myself. I want to be strong. I want to be strong. Having a family would be so good for my balance that one day I'll walk a tightrope along the guardrails of the Jacques-Cartier Bridge debating when to fall. Isn't it wonderful!

But a year before my mother and stepfather's wedding, I'm lying in my grandmother's bed. She's babysitting me. I've been watching TV all night but now I'm kind of bored. I can usually watch TV for ages: *Ciné-Quiz, Perdus dans l'espace, Fanfreluche, Picotine*,[25] the commercials, even the cooking shows. Everything flies, anything goes, and at five years old I'm a full-on TV addict jacked on entertainment headlines and Hollywood mush. You could say I frigging love TV! But tonight I'm already tired of watching TV. I'm bored because of my grandmother. Tonight she's in a bad mood. Tonight the old hag won't quit whining, and it's bugging me.

"Why does he take her to watch wrestling?" yells my grandmother. "It's a crazy sport. It's going to upset her. And then she'll have a depression and then it won't be him who'll take care of her! He's crazy! He's fucking crazy! Why does she love that man? He just wants to hurt her. And she can't even see it!"

She's been like this since I got here. She really lays into it. She lays it on thick. Her slice of reproaches is as tall as the Empire State Building. She'll butter up her reproach toast so high it will pierce the cloud God's sitting on. God's going to take her reproach toast up the ass.

"When will she learn that she's not made for all of that, marriage, family, having an apartment?" she yells. "She's always sick and on top of it her feet hurt so much that she can't spend her life on her feet standing up, cleaning and cooking for that big pig!"

That's what I heard all night long. There was no way for me to concentrate on the TV. I haven't got any supernatural powers. I can't make an abstraction of my surroundings. The slightest thing bothers me easily. Fuck, she should know! I can hardly concentrate for one minute on the same thing, she should remember. Damn! There, lying on my grandmother's bed, I'm super angry, I'm super pissed off! I'm red, I'm red, white, and blue with rage. I've got my French flag out, so it's my turn to complain. In fact, if Mémé comes back I'm going to vomit up my Camembert on her head.

She comes back.

"Shut your trap!"

"What?"

"I said, shut your trap, you old fuck!"

"What? Did I hear you right?"

"I said shut your trap, you old fuck!"

"How dare you say that to me! You're mean as hell! You're happy, eh, when I worry? You're glad when things aren't going well?"

112 | BORDERLINE

"Stop! Stop! Stop!"

"I'm in my own house and I can go on all night if I want to!"

"Stop! I can't stand it anymore!"

"If you keep being mean like that, I'm going to call your real father, Bad Daddy. He's going to bring you to his house where he lives with his whore and that won't be funny at all."

Now I'm crying. Now I'm screaming. Now it's for real. Why did she say that? Bad Daddy? Why? My body trembles like I'm sitting on a dryer. I tremble so much my freckles, nails, and teeth could fly off, I tremble like a fool but I don't know if it's because I'm only wearing my little white underpants and undershirt or because the mean old lady said Bad Daddy and it's resonating in stereo in my head— Bad Daddy, Bad Daddy, Bad Daddy—and it scares me more than the *Bonhomme Sept-Heures*, more than King Kong, more than Group A streptococcus.

It's because something really serious happened last week. Serious as a heart attack. Serious as an explosion in a daycare. Serious as a little girl drowning in a pool on a Sunday afternoon. We were walking slowly along Ontario Street, me and my two mothers. I was between the two of them and they held me by the hands. My arms in the air like an Olympic athlete who just finished their competition. I was probably thinking of the toys they'd just bought me and the fun I'd have playing with them. Then a man came along. I didn't see him but I felt him. I felt my mother's nervousness in my hand. I didn't need anything else. I knew I was in danger. I wanted them to let go of my hands so I could run away, but they were holding them too tightly. My arms were out like on a cross. An offering. The man leaned his head towards me. I knew who he was even though I could only make out a black shadow. A black shadow that smiled, because I'm sure he smiled. He said two or three words but I couldn't understand anything. I was already screaming. There were so many sparks and flames around me, as if they'd made a circle of fire to keep me from running away. So I started to squirm like a little possessed person, like the girl in *The Exorcist*. I think that at one moment my head even completely turned around and I saw behind me, where a crowd was gathering, and people were talking amongst themselves. I saw the police arrive. I saw the fish at the fishmonger's. They started to dance and make fun of me. And because the fish were moving it started to stink. And it stank. And the smell made me black out. The man came to look at my backwards face. My knees gave way. I didn't want Bad Daddy to take me away with him.

Ever since I was two years old, my grandmother told me he was bad and that if I wasn't good, he'd take me away with him. Three years of being told that causes some brain damage, there are consequences, there are certain side effects. No, he couldn't bring me with him. No. I thought I'd been good.

"I want to see my little girl," said Bad Daddy's booming voice.

"Can't you see she's having a meltdown?" yelled my grandmother. "You're scaring her! Go away! Go or I'll have you arrested!"

I could hear what they were saying but it was as if everyone was talking underwater. And I started to think that this was it, we'd all turned into fish. Montreal was a huge fishbowl. And I was a little goldfish who'd turned grey, who'd lost all its orange scales from nervousness. Bad Daddy was a big, mean catfish like the big catfish in *Démétan*.[26] The big catfish was going to take me away with him and tie up my arms and legs on a cross with big lianas, and he would pull out my belly button and tie it with another liana tied to a tree.

My two mothers started to walk fast. My legs were too weak to carry me, I couldn't keep up. So they dragged me all the way to our house. They made me run up the stairs to our apartment. I felt each step on my belly and on my thighs. Even safe, far from Bad Daddy, I kept trembling and suffocating. My grandmother took charge. She grabbed me by the arms and threw me into the bath, submerged me in bathwater. The water was very hot, but it felt freezing to me. I heard my mother weeping lamentations in her room. She cried like she cries every time she forgets to take her antidepressants. Her sobs are like long wails, they stretch out into space like hot marshmallow. Her cries are like the

BORDERLINE | 115

moans of someone who's just committed suicide who you're trying to bring back to life. Her groans are the ones she'll have in six years, lying in her bed, in another room of lamentations.

Dr. Coallier was there. I didn't even see come in. He looked at me through his glasses that always reflected all the lights in the house. Once again, I couldn't see his eyes. He looked at me and said a few words, and my grandmother turned me over. I felt a pinch in my right butt cheek. Everything slowed down. I heard, "Nervous breakdown. Nervous breakdoooown. Nerrrvous breeaaakdooown." I thought about how little fish don't have the same nervous systems as human beings, they said it the other day on TV, so fish can't have nervous breakdowns. Then I felt the piss-yellow comforter, so cushy and soft. I also saw, like in a movie, the screen that keeps the flies from coming in and the cockroaches from going out. And then everything turned into water. Montreal became a big fishpond. And I swam in the water. I swam and I swam!

"Fuck! You can't say that! You're the mean one! Mean! Mean! As mean as Cinderella's stepmother! As mean as Mrs. Olsen in *Little House on the Prairie*!"

My grandmother stops talking. She understands she's maybe gone too far. She goes to sit in the living room, in the darkness and silence. She leaves me there, in her bed. Lying under her piss-yellow comforter.

I get tired of crying after a while because it's stuffing

up my nose and having a stuffed-up nose is one of the things I hate most. So I stop crying and think of something else. I think of my mother, who, even if she were still there, in that moment, wouldn't do anything, because she'd be afraid of her mother. I think of my future stepfather, who promised to take me horse riding, and I really want to go horse riding. I think of his car, too. How much I like to lie on the back seat at night when we go for a drive, and to fall asleep watching the streetlights. On my back, rocked, safe. I think of lots of things like that, and time passes, still so slowly. Still so brutally. Then I get up and go find my grandmother. I don't want to be alone anymore. I want someone to take care of me. I want to be two. So I swallow my pride and go see my grandmother. There are times when I want to be with others so badly, I'd turn myself into a Hare Krishna with shaved head and bells on my toes just to not be alone. I'm like that. I'm a little domesticated animal. They tamed me with sour candies and Fisher-Price toys. I was sold to the highest bidder. The first stranger who offered me candy, I'd get into his car without asking any questions. That's the way it is. I have my own welfare at heart; you'd better believe it.

My grandmother's sitting in the silent darkness of her living room, like I knew she would be. She's sitting by the window. Her legs are crossed. She's leaning against the arm of her rough brown sofa. Her eyes are moist. She's been crying. They're probably crocodile tears. You could fill a suitcase with them. It seems like my grandmother never cries for real. It's like she's always pretending, like she's staring at some bright point somewhere on the floor until her eyes start to prickle, or as if she'd rubbed some soap in her eyes, or as if she'd secretly been breathing onions. That's the kind of thing I do when I want toys. But she does it to make people feel guilty. To make guilt gnaw at us, from the tips of our toes to the roots of our hair, to make guilt burrow into our bones so we'll depend on her, fuck.

"Will you tell me a story, Mémé?"

"So. You can't sleep?"

"No."

"Okay. Come on, let's go to the bedroom."

In the bedroom, both of us lying in her bed, wrapped in her piss-yellow comforter, my grandmother reads me my favourite story: *Cinderella*.

"Once upon a time, a pretty little blonde girl lived with her father and..."

The words seem to fall from the sky in a shimmering rain. Everything becomes magical. Everything becomes a fairyland. From the first sentence, my identification is complete. I'm Cinderella. Disney's beautiful Cinderella, whose family pisses her off but who, one day, will make the comeback of a lifetime. I'll also make a comeback, and all those who pissed me off will pay.

"Her stepmother and her two mean stepsisters didn't

love her and often laughed at her . . . "

"Mémé, sometimes you're mean like that."

"Come on, I don't laugh at you."

"No, but you make me cry."

"I'm only mean because I want what's best for you. But I'm not actually that mean. There are children who are badly treated. No one feeds them. No one dresses them. They get tied up and burned with cigarettes. That's how people have fun with them."

"Have fun with them? Isn't it fun to have fun with someone?"

"Not having fun with toys, having fun with someone. You know, touching someone everywhere, even where you're not supposed to."

"Where are you not supposed to touch?"

"In your bum!"

Then my grandmother starts her prattle. She butters me, she coddles me, she'd cook me if she could. Come here, my chicken, come here where it's nice and warm! She'd put a big onion in my mouth and she'd cook me at 350 degrees Celsius for two and a half hours, enough time to make me tender from all the stories she tells me. My grandmother wants me to say things, she wants me to admit things she's invented. She wants me to tell her lies: lies that will make her happy and make her smile. Enormous lies that will make her life beautiful, make her believe she's not alone in her crusade against all of my mother's lovers. My grandmother wants me to say things that I don't want to say, that I can't say.

I try to change the subject by telling her everything that goes through my head. *Hey, Mémé! I'm hungry! Hey, Mémé, I'm itchy all over! There's a ghost in the hallway!* But she keeps coming back to her prattle, hanging on my words like a journalist in the middle of an interview who will crack the story. She wants to hound me until I tell her the lie she wants to hear.

"Did he ever scratch you, your mother's new boyfriend?"

"Of course, he's scratched me!"

"Oh, yeah, how?"

"Like this, with his fingers."

"Oh, yeah? And where did he do that?"

"On my back and on my head, too."

"Did he ever scratch you anywhere else?"

"I don't remember."

"Or is it that you don't want to tell me?"

"You're so annoying! I already told you he's scratched me my back and my head. I don't tell lies."

She continues. She won't let up. She's relentless. I don't want to say anything bad about my mother's boyfriend. I think my mother's boyfriend is pretty nice. He spoils me, he buys me tons of stuff. He often takes us out to the Chinese restaurant. I like eating at the Chinese restaurant. My grandmother would never take us there. She's convinced Chinese people cook rats, cats, and pigeons, and they mix them into their bacteria egg rolls to make us sick. She's convinced Chinese people are massacring us through our stomachs, wreaking havoc on us, and that's how they're going to take over the world. That's what she thinks.

My mother's boyfriend takes me for drives in his car and that's better than anything. I need it. I need to be taken out for drives: he and my mother sitting in the front and me all alone in the back, lying down, watching the streetlights and hoping to catch sight of a flying saucer in the sky. My grandmother would never take us for a drive in a car, she doesn't have one. She's too poor. Her husband didn't leave her anything when he died except regrets and an unflagging desire to erase him. The first thing my grandmother said when my grandfather died was: good riddance! Then she threw out everything that belonged to him, destroyed all the furniture they'd bought over the years. She also tore up all the photos he was in. And when he was photographed with me or with my mother, she cut the pictures up and threw out the parts where he was. Now most of our photos are all cut up into little pieces and there are only pictures of my mother and me. Our photo album looks rough as hell!

One hour, two hours, three hours with her prattle, I go soft as butter and finally tell her what she wants to hear.

"Yes, he touched me. He put cotton balls in my bum!"

Now she's happy. She smiles with all her teeth. There, that's it, she thinks she'll be able to control my mother's

BORDERLINE | 121

future. She thinks she can keep my mother by her side, handy, all her life, to take care of her in her old age. I look at her being happy and it makes me feel funny. She looks like a little girl on Christmas morning who got the doll of her dreams. I don't know what I look like in all of this. I don't know why I said that, either, cotton balls in the bum! I don't even know what it is! Anyway, yes. The moment I opened my mouth to talk I thought of a commercial for toilet paper. And there it came out: cotton balls. Cotton balls! Creation in a time of war. Now I look like a good little cotton ball.

"You can't tell anyone what I just said, Mémé."

"But of course I can! It's for your own good if I tell your mother. He's bad, that man. If we don't stop him, he'll take you away, you and your mother, he will take you very far away to rape and kill you. And no one will find you because he'll leave you in a field, at night, without any light. We have to stop him! We have to stop him!"

My grandmother stares off into the distance and nods her head at her crackpot plan. Her lips move. She's talking to herself. She looks crazy. Someone should lock her up, like they did with my mother. Crazy people have to be locked up. Otherwise they contaminate others. Craziness is contagious, I know. My grandmother is free but I'm the one who's been conditioned. And my condition at the moment is undefined, indefinite. In fact, I don't count anymore. Mémé has completely lost interest in her little monkey. I

122 | BORDERLINE

said what she wanted to hear. I might choke on my guilt, she wouldn't care a bit. I don't interest her anymore. I'm not part of her plans.

Later, when my mother and her boyfriend get back from the Roland-Robitaille Centre, my grandmother will try to stab the couple with her words. There will be screaming, there will be crying, things are going to fly. I'll be so scared that, in my nervousness, I'll manage to move the big dresser that weighs two thousand pounds in my grandmother's room to hide behind. My grandmother will throw all the dishes from the cupboard. My mother will roll herself into a little ball on the floor and cry. In the left corner of the kitchen, by the door. My future stepfather will yell for a long time, then leave, slamming the door. The glass on the door will smash. The icy winter wind will sift into the house and make the curtains and all the loose papers flutter. Under the big yellow light bulb, so bright it burns your eyes, the apartment will look like an abandoned house that turns any travellers who visit mad.

That night my mother and I won't sleep. A white night. The only time in all my life. A white night. After my grandmother calms down and retires into the darkness of the living room, I'll come out of hiding, from behind the dresser that weighed two thousand pounds, to join my mother. First, I'll pull on her left arm, so she'll follow me. I'll say to her: *Môman! Môman! Come with me behind the dresser, we'll be safe. Môman! Come on! Come on!* She'll look

BORDERLINE | 123

at me and continue to cry all the tears of her body, and oh my God she has so many! My mother cries all the time, it must be her antidepressants, they must enlarge her tear ducts. Seeing that she's not following me I'll pull on both her arms and say at the same time, *Môman! Come behind the dresser! We'll be safe! Follow me! Please! Môman* . . . She still won't move. So I'll sit beside her and wait. And wait, I don't know what for. But I'll wait with her, curled up in a little ball. We'll sit together on the kitchen floor, muddy from our winter boots.

In a year my mother will marry my stepfather anyway, the restaurant meals and the car trips will be fine despite my cotton ball story, but only for a few months, a passing lull. Amnesty will prove deceptive. False. It's my fault. I sold my country to the enemy for a little peace. I'm a little renegade, a little traitor, a pretty little five-year-old Judas. From then on, my games won't know any limits and I'll be at war against humanity, but especially against myself.

Chapter 9:

La Ronde

For Éric Villeneuve, who always smiled and who, on April 24th, 1998 (three days ago), at twenty-seven years old ... Anxiolytics and a plastic bag over his head. Like that Peter Gabriel song you transcribed for me, Éric. "Oh! Here comes the flood ... We will say goodbye to flesh and blood."

Her eyes open and shut. She's almost unconscious, but she's holding my hand, so she knows I'm here. She doesn't say a word. I don't say a word. I can't. I've forgotten how speaking works. I'm being strangled from within. I can't remember how to open my mouth. I can't remember how to breathe. I hiccup. With every breath, my throat brings up pieces of my oesophagus. My throat is burning. Everything is burning. Everywhere. As much within me as without. Even the walls are burning. Everything looks red. Red with lightning that ricochets everywhere I look. I'm seeing life through a kaleidoscope. Like when I was eleven years old. I have to get up and call emergency for help, but she doesn't want me to and she holds my hand so firmly I can't pull it back. She never wanted to go to the hospital. She says that doctors are worse than Nazis. So I stay beside her. Not sitting or standing, something between the two.

Folded over myself as if I have a bad stomachache. I look at her without seeing what's happening. But what exactly is happening? My grandmother is lying in front of me: she makes a death rattle. She has more and more difficulty breathing. She is so old. Ninety-eight years old, that's old for a grandmother. It's too old. But still, she's young. She's as young as I am. It wasn't that long ago we played badminton together. And she won. I let her beat me because she liked winning and smiled all night. She gave me cookies and I smiled. If I could, Mémé, I'd give you twenty years of my life. No, thirty, forty, one hundred years of my life, I don't care enough for my own. The blade is never far from my veins. The blade that'll open my veins lengthwise so I don't miss my shot.

She groans. She holds my hand more and more loosely. I want to call the ER or 911 but she doesn't want me to and holds my hand.

"Mémé. No. Please! Hold on...a little...just a few more years...Môman...Mémé...Môman...Let me call the hospital. They can save you..."

She's still groaning. Her mouth is wide open. It's ugly. Her mouth is frightening. Her mouth and her body. She's so thin. She's as thin as Mr. Burns in *The Simpsons*. She's been fading before my eyes. Her fat seems to free-fall through space. My grandmother is fleeing the Earth one fat particle at a time. Maybe I should wrap her in cellophane to keep her from leaving, to keep her by me? She's my only family. The only link that truly holds me to this goddamned planet, to this goddamned life...

"Mémé...Please, hold on...Do it for me. I can't breathe when you're not here, I can't do this alone. I'm way too scared. I'm much too young for you to leave me. Look at my hand, it's a baby hand that never touched anything bad...Look at my fine hair, my baby hair you still have to wash with baby shampoo. I can't even walk alone without making mistakes, you know..."

The umbilical cord that ties me to my mother is about to be severed. There isn't enough air. I won't be able to survive, I know that too well. I won't be able to. Manage it. Because I'm not weaned yet. The foetus forgotten on the dirty floor grew up too fast. I need my walker, I need my bottle, I need my pacifier, I need my placenta. I need to regress a little.

"Mémé, don't go! I need you to tell me some crap, I need you to yell at me, I don't know. Remember when I was little, we watched movies on Radio-Québec on Saturday nights, the Fellini movies. At the time I didn't know who Fellini was, and you didn't either. Anyway, you never gave a shit who he was, but you liked the stories. I never felt alone. You were there, sitting beside me, on the dirty old checked sofa that smelled like cat piss. Your hands rested flat against your thighs, your fingers moving lightly, a nervous tic. You're nervous, too. Like me. Nervous. The drama that's constantly circling overhead. That feeling of guilt that you always wore so uneasily. Dealt with so badly. Two dead children. One and a half years old and six months. Two little girls. That's why you smother me and that's why you smothered my mother . . . Mémé, you have to stay alive. Do it for me."

She's stopped groaning.

❀ ❀ ❀

Only one heart beats in the house, but the noise is so loud the walls tremble, the wallpaper unfurls, the floor caves. But the blood in my overly dilated veins flows calmly. It breathes. Without too much effort. And one heart still beats. Mine. Will I ever wake from this nightmare? In the meantime, I have to unknot my nerves, my nerves from her nerves. I have to put the nerves back into the little blonde girl. She's been waiting for them for such a long time. She's always following me. It can't be easy for her. I have to be understanding. She watches me. She's so little. Still, she looks so sure of herself. Something of my grand-mother lives on in her eyes. In fact, she has my grand-mother's eyes from before they looked like monkey eyes. Grey monkey eyes. She has big eyes. I was always told that I had my grandmother's eyes that she had when she was young. Big eyes. I've always been told I had my grand-mother's temperament. And her big eyes. I want to put the nerves back inside the little blonde girl, except my dead grandmother's holding my hand too tightly for me to get away. So I make a motion to the little girl to come back later. I'll give them back to her then.

My hand still gripping my grandmother's, I lie by her side and look at her. She has a nice nose. A nice Cleopatra nose. I've often been told that I have a Cleopatra nose, so I must have my grandmother's nose. I look like her. Well, I looked like her, since she's gone.

My grandmother is dead.

Mémé, did I ever tell you about the most beautiful death I ever saw? A seagull in front of the house. Its big, open beak tried to catch a last breath that never came. It rested its head on one open wing, then the other. Graceful wings that made...graceful ballerina movements. And those little kids ruined its beautiful death with their sticks. Mémé, please...take me with you. I hate myself so much. I should have done something to keep you from dying. I should have...Mémé...You didn't understand. I always wanted to be your superhero. Look, Mémé, if you pull your hand away, I'll be able to show you...the costume is just under my dress. The blue superhero costume with the big red cape...You'll see, Mémé, I'll be your superhero and I'll save you. I'll take you in my arms and we'll fly away to some other place. I'll protect you from all possible crashes, from every possible end of the world. But give me a chance, Mémé...

⁂

It's daylight. I slept. A long time. I don't know how long. It's daylight. I open my eyes. It smells bad. It's Mémé who smells. I smell, too. My grandmother's odour has seeped into my clothes, into my skin, into my hair. I fell asleep against her. Something I haven't done in such a long time, since I was a little girl. I smell like death. I smell like Hygrade sausage roasted in the oven, I always thought that smelled like death, little roasted sausages in a frying pan. So I called them little death sausages. My grandmother smells like a little death sausage. What will become of me? My grandmother was perpetually in my head, she was my inner voice, her eyes watched me all the time. I've been linked to her for so long that I've forgotten how to think, that's why my thoughts are spinning like tops in my head; I forgot how to love, that's why love runs out from between my legs, from between my thighs; I forgot how to be. Be. What will become of me? I was raised by wrecks. I always knew that I was poor, even nature was forbidden. Just like it was forbidden to forget me. To forget me. I lost my lightness years ago, I'm inhabited by kilolitres of sadness that also runs out between my legs. I'm leaking out of my vagina. That's why I'm so easily excited.

I look outside. It's raining. I swallow the window that's crying. I'm going to leave. My grandmother grips my hand firmly. With one quick move I am able to untangle myself. There's a crack. A horrible sound. Like when someone whose knees are shot squats.

"I'm sorry, Mémé, I didn't want to hurt you. I never wanted to hurt you. Now I have to go. I have to leave you in order to find you better. You chose to die here. I've chosen to die elsewhere. I'm sorry. We won't have a family mausoleum. Anyway, you always said that I didn't have enough family spirit and that was a good thing. You were proud of me for that. Proud. Come to think of it, you never told me you were proud of me. No, you told others you were proud of me because I wasn't family-oriented, but you never told me directly. You never paid me any compliments, either . . . Yes, true, you did say I was pretty, once. It was the one thing you told me: a pretty woman. But you added that I ruined everything because I was pretty. You said my beauty was my curse. Well, my beauty is done cursing me because I'm going to give my beauty to you, Mémé, I'm going to give it to you. It's just a question of time.

I leave the house. I walk in the street. I walk like a crazy person. I don't know if it's because I'm walking like a crazy person that everyone's staring at me or if it's because I've been wearing the same clothes for two days; my clothes that smell like little death sausages. My wrinkled clothes.

Luckily, they don't look too wrinkled because I'm dressed entirely in black. Ever since I was five years old, I've dressed head-to-toe in black, as if I was in mourning. I am in mourning, and I was even before my grandmother died. I was in mourning before I was even born, because I was born without a family. Nothing. My mother had me when she was in a medicated bubble. It took a lot to make me cry: one slap, two slaps, three slaps. I was numb, in a medicated bubble, too. Baby addict. I was going to be addicted to nicotine patches. I was going to have to quit smoking. Have to quit running around. Quit drinking. Quit. Spend my life trying not to be dependant. Spend my life in mourning. In mourning. Black adorns and inhabits me. Black, on me, becomes pure evil. Black clothes. Black is beautiful, makes me beautiful. One day the king had to take a wife. Two wives were offered to him. For better and for worse. A nice one and a mean one. For better or for worse. You have to make the right choice. A king's life can be long. In order to make the perfect choice, he asked the palace painter, who must surely have been a French painter because he was always yelling like my ex-boyfriend, to make a painting of his two would-be wives. Two paintings from which he would perform the final gesture, the ball and chain around his foot secure. The painter, like all good artists, had a feeling for people. So he painted the mean woman surrounded by an amalgam of colours and he painted the nice woman against a black background.

The mean woman's face was lost amongst all the colours, while the nice woman's face was highlighted by the black background. The king chose the kind, nice woman and he married her.

I always wanted to be the one who was chosen, the nice one. I always wanted to be the one who was noticed, the seductress, the *Belle de Nuit*. I never wanted to be the one left behind. But there, it's happened. Later, I'll put some colour on my black clothes. Nice, living colour.

I walk quickly down the street. Curiously, I don't stumble. I walk with a steadfast pace. I don't know where I'm going, but I move forward and get out of breath, that's the point. The weather is grey and heavy as concrete. It's warm and humid. I'm sweating like a pig. Usually I think I'm pretty in this kind of weather but now I don't care. I don't care because I'm leaving my beauty little by little. I'm readying myself for another bereavement. In fact, it'll be more of an offering for my Mémé, she'll be happy.

You'll be happy, eh, Mémé?

People plough into me. It's as though they don't see me, as though I'm transparent. Unless I'm the one bumping into them? I don't know. The light is too bright, as if it's following me everywhere, as if it wanted me to admit something. I'm not walking anymore, I'm running. I'm running from the light. Its clarity is violent, painful, it breaks my skin. I'm running, running, I turn down an alleyway, shove myself under some cardboard boxes that have been left outside. I have to protect myself from the light, otherwise everyone will be able to read me, everyone will read my thoughts, and I don't want that. I don't want them to find me. I'm full of poison. I killed my mother. I killed my grandmother. I destroy everything I touch. I'm a rose with thorns, even my petals have thorns.

The sun won't stop shining. Its rays are like swords that try to pierce me. I can't think anymore. Concentrate. Concentrate. There, over there. Graffiti on the wall. There's graffiti on the wall right there, in front of me, in front of my cardboard boxes. It's full of colours: pink, red, green. Graffiti. Concentrate. Graffiti. Can't panic. Can't. Why isn't the little blonde girl here? Graffiti. She could help me. Graffiti. Pink, red, with some green. The light is too bright. I can't have a nervous breakdown, no, not me. Not me. Close your eyes. Graffiti. Shh! Shh!

❁ ❁ ❁

Little children all around me.

"Go away! Go away!"

They stare at me. What happened? I think I fainted. How long have I been here? It's dark. I remember the light that was trying to rape me. I remember the people who walked all over me. I remember death. Hey, I can't forget my plan . . . I need money.

"Go away, all of you! I'm not a dying seagull, you won't get me. Go away! Go away!"

The kids disperse, and I crawl out of my shelter. I come out of my lethargy. I can't let myself go. No more carelessness. There's something I have to do.

"Antoine."

"Sissi, is that you, where are you? What's the matter?"

"Antoine..."

"What's the matter, Sissi?"

"Antoine..."

"Sissi, are you going to tell me what's the matter?"

"My grandmother... my grandmother, my mother... died."

"Oh! Wait for me, Sissi, I'm coming. Where are you?"

"Antoine, I hope I suffocate. Suffocate. You can't come. I don't want to hurt you, you understood me. I hurt everyone. Give me some money, I have to bury my grandmother."

"I'm coming, Sissi..."

"You don't get it! I want money! I want to bury my grandmother, but I don't want to see you, I don't want to hurt you. Send me some money, that's all I want! Put it in my account."

"But the banks are closed, Sissi... How can I help...?"

I hang up. I have to call someone else, quick. I need money, but who? Who?

"Éric, it's Sissi."

"Hey! I haven't heard from you in ages."
"Uh-huh."
"What's up with you? I've missed you. Why did you disappear like that? Why did you do that? How come?"
"Éric, my grandmother died. I need money to bury her."
"Hang on, I'll lend you some."
"Éric, can you help me? I'm also going to need a place to sleep. Can you put me up in a hotel room for tonight?"
"Of course! Where can I meet you?"
"In front of the Château de l'Argoat Hotel."

It starts all over again. I feel like I've lived this moment a thousand times. I'm lying on a bed in a hotel room. But now I know the room number: 13. I asked for it, I insisted on it. It's the number of misfortune. It's an unlucky number, 13, and I'm unlucky. I also know the name of the hotel, Château de l'Argoat. A castle for Princess Sissi. A castle in the sky for a fallen Cinderella. Cinderella was always my favourite fairy tale. I don't know how many times I read it or how many times my Mémé read it to me: a hundred times, two hundred, a thousand. I always wanted to be Cinderella and have Prince Charming whisk me away from my tragic kingdom. But princes...Antoine was there for a while, until I wrecked everything. And Éric, a prince? No. A big frog that jiggles in bed. Naked, fat, sticky.

I'm lying on the bed. Éric crawls towards me to lie on my body. He spreads over me. He's heavy. I feel like a Salem witch being buried alive under enormous rocks. Go ahead, crush me. I want to suffocate. I close my eyes. He moves, puts his hands everywhere, kisses my skin—it hardly belongs to me. He breathes hard. My grandmother groaned. He breathes and emits the strange sounds of a rutting animal. It's ugly. I prefer my grandmother's death rattle. His hands search everywhere and distract me. His hands and his breathing. I haven't had anything to drink. For once, I forgot to drink. Reality is painful. His fingers go into all the holes they find. They're sliding everywhere. I'm tired. I wish I was lying beside my Mémé. I still smell like death. And he doesn't stop sniffing me. The smell of death must excite him.

He turns me over. He wants me to be on top of him. He wants me to sit on his big belly. He wants to look at me. He wants to watch my little body that has grown thinner and thinner. My little body that has less and less shape. He would like me to look at him. *Look at me, Sissi.* But I can't. *Open your eyes, Sissi.* I force myself to open my eyes. I look all around the room, everywhere except at him. Everything is white. The walls are white, the sheets are white, the curtains are white. Absolutely everything.

Except him. Éric tries to get inside me, I close my legs. I can't. I can't anymore.

"Éric, go away."

"But...but..."

"Please go away. I need to be alone...for a while. Please!"

Éric gets up without saying anything. Looking like a beaten dog. Flaccid tail between his legs. Looking like the same guy who fucked me in this same hotel a few years ago. Now I'm lying on the bed in room number 13 of the Château de l'Argoat and I'm not crying. My eyes are dry as autumn leaves, like the ones you see in ads for hydrating cream. You were right, Mémé, my beauty is deserting me.

I get up. I go to the mirror to look at myself. I see my face as if from behind a veil. I'm lit by the reflections of the Moon. My long, dishevelled blonde hair falls in a disorderly way over my shoulders, it looks like curtains, curtains framing my sad face. This sad face needs cheering up. I'm too young to be sad. Too young. Twenty-six years old. But like I'm a hundred, my life is so heavy to drag around.

Bang! A fist to the mirror! The mirror shatters into a thousand pieces that don't fall. I look at myself, my face looks like a puzzle now. I take out part of my left shoulder. I will try to brighten this sad face. I press the piece of shattered mirror against my lips. I draw myself a laughing mouth. A nice, laughing mouth. The mirror is like a blade,

I stretch the lines of the lips into the middle of my cheeks. First the left cheek then the right. I apply myself. Both sides very evenly. It's important. I like symmetry. Even as a little girl I drew with a lot of symmetry. My mother told me: *You spent hours on your drawings. You were good at drawing. You could have become a great illustrator.* Well look, Môman, I'm still good at drawing! Look, I'm tracing a nice clown face like when I was little. You always said I was good at drawing clowns, pretty little girl clowns like me. Pretty little girl clowns with big mouths.

Blood dribbles down my chin. A little red stream trickles into my long blonde hair. The meat colour is pretty. I look at myself in the mirror. The little blonde girl also looks at me in the mirror. She's there, behind me.

"You came back!"

She doesn't answer me. She indicates that something's missing on my face. My new image isn't an exact representation of who I am. You can't fool a mirror. I never had a happy face, so my happy clown face rings false. I apply the piece of mirror beneath my left eye and trace a long, very straight tear. Then I do the same under my right eye. There...There, that's better! That's well done! I'm a sad clown but I'm smiling. The little girl looks at me, and she smiles, too.

There's far too much blood running now, and it annoys me. I shake myself. Blood spatters all over the nice white room. I think it's too bad for the cleaning lady. She's going

to have to scrub. Blood doesn't wash out easily. The red
will turn brown, then yellow. I shake myself a little again.
It's burning more and more. I have to cool off. I need to
get some air. I have to show off my new beauty, my new
ugliness. I can't stay here. I can't wait to see people's re-
actions when they see me. I'm excited. And shit! It keeps
burning.

But where can a sad clown go? To La Ronde,[27] obvi-
ously. I want to go to La Ronde. My place is the circus fair
with the animals and the monsters. I'm a monster now,
too. A nice little skinny, docile monster who laughs and
cries at the same time. A two-faced face.

I leave the hotel and walk along Sherbrooke Street.
There aren't too many people around at this hour. They
must be busy making love or making war. Too bad! I won't
know what effect I'm having. I walk. The streetlights shine
so bright they're almost like projectors. It's like I'm giving
a show, I look like a Big Rock Star. I turn on Amherst
Street.[28] I want to see people but the only people I see are
the homeless bums with discomfited attitudes. They look
more ravaged than I do. The junkies don't dare ask me
for money. I think they understand, from their globby
cloud, the story written on my face. I keep walking: one
step, two steps, three steps. It's burning me. I'm dizzy
but I keep walking. I'm not alone, the little blonde girl is
accompanying me. With me. She smiles. She looks excited.
She can't wait to get to La Ronde. I was excited too, when

I was a little girl going to La Ronde. I couldn't wait to get on the rides, to take a turn on the roller coaster and the Ferris wheel. My stepfather always tried to win stuffed animals for me, but especially for his pride. He would waste part of his paycheque under my mother's bewildered eyes to win a hideous stuffed animal that would wind up in the dusty, humid shed.

When I get to Papineau Street I see the Jacques-Cartier Bridge. It seems to be crumbling beneath the weight of the stars. They're super bright tonight. My grandmother must be there. She must be shining brightly right now, too. She must be happy because my beauty can't ruin me anymore. She must be proud of me, if she sees me, her vision was never very good.

It's a beautiful summer night. A very beautiful summer night. My grandmother must be happy in heaven. It must be cool up there. I walk along the bridge's sidewalk. The further I walk, the less the air is polluted, the more the wind blows. It feels good on my cuts. The little girl is still there, at my side, and she smiles up at me. We're holding each other's hands on the bridge and we're walking briskly. It's good, I don't feel alone. It's very good. Halfway across, I can see the lights of La Ronde. Most of them are out. La Ronde is closing. Oh no! That's not good! I really want to go on the Ferris wheel and touch the stars, and now I won't be able to. I've failed, and I can't take it anymore. Nothing ever works out. I have no control over my

BORDERLINE | 141

life or what happens. I'm fed up. I have to touch the stars. My grandmother has to see my new face up close. She can't see very well. I can't handle another failure. Maybe if I throw myself into the river, I'll reach the stars, and my grandmother will be able to see me. The shock of my free-fall will be hard on my body. But it doesn't matter because the more I hurt, the more I'll feel I'm reaching the stars. All right, now's the time. I have to do it quickly. Drivers are stopping to see what's going on. All right, a jump into the air and I'll touch the stars. A jump into the air and I'll join my grandmother.

Epilogue

The scars barely show, now. The story written on my face fades. Turn the page at the sound of the bell. The book is closed. Cinderella is still as fragile as her glass slipper. Very fragile. All the mirrors of her palace were taken away, and the knives from the drawers, too, just in case. You have to beware of princesses, they're only cartoons. One moment they're dead, then, in the next scene, they've come back to life, they're married and have children, and they live happily ever after. I don't think I'll have any children, at least not for now. That's what my shrink, slumped in a chair, counselled me. That's what she said, because it's a she, it's a young woman. A beautiful fairy godmother who dresses in Jacob and Gap. She has the big eyes of a Japanese anime character and a voice that lays its hand on my jittery skull. A beautiful, soft voice like the song of the stars. Because stars sing. I know it. I heard them, one summer night.

Princes also exist. Except they don't necessarily arrive on a flying white horse, but on a Voyageur[29] bus, like the sexual angel with the broken wings I met after I left the hospital. They don't have shining, unmuddied clothes, either. No. They can wear Pantera sweaters, and forget to wash, but it doesn't take anything away from their charm. And with your eyes closed, lying naked in bed with a prince, you can't tell the difference.

Montreal, December 29, 1998.

Notes:

1. Quebec dialect, or *joual*, derived from the English word "bone-setter," an archaic word for "doctor." Now used to mean "bogeyman."

2. A dépanneur is a corner store, a bodega.

3. Now discontinued, Softimage was a 3D computer graphics application used to produce 3D computer graphics, 3D modelling, and computer animation.

4. Cégep is a network of publicly funded preuniversity and technical colleges in Quebec. Originally a French acronym for Collège d'enseignement général et professionnel, it is now considered a word in itself.

5. In Quebec people colloquially refer to apartments as a one-and-a-half, meaning a studio apartment, a two-and-a-half, meaning a one-bedroom, and so on. (The half is the bathroom.)

6. Régent Ducharme, 1941–2017, was a Montreal-based novelist and playwright. His novel, *Le nez qui voque*, was published in 1967.

7. From 1973 to 1977, Télé-Métropole aired *Les tannants*, a late-afternoon variety program hosted by Pierre Marcotte, Joël Denis, and Shirley Théroux.

8. Roger Giguère, born in 1945, is a Quebec comedian, puppeteer, and sound effects engineer.

9. Shirley Théroux, born in 1945, is a Quebec singer and television host.

10. Pierre Marcotte, born in 1938, is a Quebec television host and businessperson.

11. Michel Courtemanche, born in 1964, is a Quebec comedian, actor, and television producer.

12. *Surpise Surprise* was a hidden camera television show conceived by Quebec comedian Marcel Béliveau, first broadcast in September 1987.

13. *Emmanuelle*: a series of mostly French erotic films and TV movies whose main character is inspired by the character created by Emmanuelle Arsan in her 1959 novel *Emmanuelle*.

14. In Quebec, a local community service centre (CLSC) is a public organization offering front-line health services and assistance with services such as home care for seniors and people with disabilities, prenatal classes, newborn care, vaccination of young children, health and hygiene training services in schools, etc.

15. A song by Cajun singer and songwriter, Zachary Richard. Not unlike "The Old Lady Who Swallowed a Fly," the song is about how everything is in everything. The words are: "L'amour est dans le cœur / Et le cœur est dans l'oiseau / Et l'oiseau est dans l'œuf / Et l'œuf est dans le nid / Et le nid est dans le trou / Et le trou est dans le nœud / Et le nœud est dans la branche / Et la branche est dans l'arbre..." Zachary Richard was born in Louisiana in 1950.

16. Sounds like "la broche" — "the staple."

17. Sounds like "la brosse" — "the brush."

18. "La brèche" means "the breach, the gap, or the crack."

19. Founded in 1917, Steinberg's Supermarkets was a Quebec company that, at its peak, operated a grocery chain, a department store chain, and a housing stock. It went bankrupt in 1992.

20. Bernard Derome, CM, OQ, born in 1944, was the news anchor for the weeknight edition of *Le Téléjournal* from 1970 to 1988.

21. Traditional French lullaby. Any child's name can be injected into the lyrics to personalize the song.

22. Hubert Aquin, 1929-1977, a Quebec novelist, essayist, filmmaker, political activist, and editor.

23. *UFO Robot Grendizer*, also known as *Force Five: Grandizer* in the United States, is a Japanese super robot anime television series and manga created by manga artist Go Nagai. It was especially popular in France and Quebec, as well as among French-speaking Canadians in New Brunswick, where it aired as *Goldorak*.

24. An allusion to the novel, *Il pleut des rats* by David Homel, Acte Sud, 1992. Translated into English as *Rat Palms*, HarperCollins, 1993.

25. *Ciné-Quiz* was a quiz segment that aired during TV movies that allowed viewers to win prizes. *Perdus dans l'espace* is the dubbed version of *Lost in Space*. *Fanfreluche*, a children's television show made in Quebec by Radio-Canada, ran from 1968 to 1971. *Picotine*, a television show made in Quebec by Radio-Canada, ran from 1972 to 1975.

26. A Japanese anime about a frog named Démétan. The show aired in Quebec from 1982 to 1986.

27. La Ronde is an amusement park just off the island of Montreal.

28. Rue Amherst is now rue Atateken, the Mowhawk word for "brotherhood and sisterhood."

29. Voyageur Bus Lines, known as Voyageur, is a Canadian intercity bus company that serves Eastern Ontario and Western Quebec.

ABOUT THE AUTHOR

Marie-Sissi Labrèche is the author of seven books and her work has also been featured in such publications as *Stop, XYZ, Nouvelles fraiches*, and in the anthology *Folles frues fortes* (Éditions Tête première 2019). *Borderline*, her first novel, was published in 2000 by Éditions Boréal, and has since been translated into German, Russian, Dutch, and Greek. Labrèche co-authored the script for the movie *Borderline*, adapted from her first two novels (Max Films), which won a Genie, four Jutras, and multiple international film prizes. Her other works include *La Brèche* (Éditions Boréal, 2002), *Montréal, la marge au coeur* (Éditions Autrement, 2004), *La lune dans un HLM* (Éditions Boréal 2006), *Psy malgré moi* (Éditions de la Courte Échelle, 2009), *Amour et autres violences* (Éditions Boréal, 2012), and *La Vie sur Mars* (Éditions Leméac, 2014). She lives in Montreal.

ABOUT THE TRANSLATOR

Melissa Bull is a writer and editor, as well as a French-to-English translator of fiction, essays, and plays. She is the editor of *Maisonneuve* magazine's "Writing from Quebec" column and has published her poetry, essays, articles, and interviews in a variety of publications including *Event*, *Lemon Hound*, *subTerrain*, *Prism,* and *Matrix*. Her translation of Nelly Arcan's *Burqa de chair* was published by Anvil Press in 2014 and her debut collection of poetry, *Rue*, was published in 2015. Melissa's first collection of short stories, *The Knockoff Eclipse*, was published in 2018 and was translated into French by Éditions Boréal in 2020. She lives in Montreal.